Face-to-Face with the Enemy

Wow, what an interrogation! I had extracted vital information from the cat, and now it was time to put it to work. I fired up engines one and two, and went roaring up to the machine shed. I wasn't one bit afraid of that Phantom Cow, but...okay, I was afraid of the old hag. Hey, she'd been recruited by the Charlies and I needed Cowboy Backup.

I cut the engines, coasted into the barn, and sent out a blast of Three Alarm Barking. Only then did I realize that I had blundered into an extremely dangerous situation. What I saw... do I dare describe this? I guess I will, but hang on to something solid.

The Return of the Charlie Monsters

John R. Erickson

Illustrations by Gerald L. Holmes

Maverick Books, Inc.

MAVERICK BOOKS, INC.
Published by Maverick Books, Inc.
P.O. Box 549, Perryton, TX 79070
Phone: 806.435.7611
www.hankthecowdog.com

First published in the United States of America by Maverick Books, Inc. 2014.

1 3 5 7 9 10 8 6 4 2

LIBRARY OF CONGRESS CONTROL NUMBER: 2014931260

978-1-59188-163-6 (paperback); 978-1-59188-263-3 (hardcover)

Hank the Cowdog® is a registered trademark of John R. Erickson.

Printed in the United States of America

To Scot and Tina,
May God bless their marriage.

CONTENTS

Case Number
RA-VS 2335

It's me again, Hank the Cowdog. When the sun came up that morning, I had no idea what lay ahead—that we would face a full-scale, two-pronged invasion by the Charlie Monsters, that they would try to bump me off with a poisoned egg, or that my relationship with Sally May would hit an all-time low.

What we're looking at here is one of the scariest stories of my whole career, but before we go any farther, let's take care of some ranch business. See, once we get into the scary parts, I might forget to tell you that this is Case Number RA-VS 2335.

It's important that you know the case number and maybe you're wondering why it's so important.

The answer might surprise you. It's so important, I can't tell you why it's so important. It's Classified Information, and we're talking about a Heavy Duty Keep-Your-Trap-Shut kind of secret.

All you need to know is that the Security Division has a numbering system and we keep records on all our cases. We're allowed to reveal the case number and that's about it. If you're okay with that, we'll move along. Ready?

Okay, in our filing system, "RA-VS" is shorthand for "Red Alert, Very Serious" and the number "2335" tells us that it happened after Case #2334 and before Case #2336. Do you get it? Case 2335 occurred in between Case 2334 and Case 2336.

The "dash" between RA and VS doesn't mean anything dark or mysterious. We put it there because...I'm not sure why we put it there. Maybe it breaks the monotony of having four letters in a row: "RAVS." Also, it makes it sound more official when we say, "This is Case Number RA-**dash**-VS 2335."

You have to admit that it's a pretty slick system. I mean, a lot of your ordinary mutts just slop through life and never keep a good set of records. On my outfit, we keep track of every little detail. For example, at this very moment, even as we speak, a flea is creeping around in the region of my left armpit. In fact...

Hee hee! It tickles. Okay, this information will go into our data files, including my response. Pay close attention. I will now sit on the ground, hike up my left hind leg, and use the claws of my left rear paw to hack the flea into salad and smithereens. Death to all fleas!

Hack, hack, hack!

Pay special attention to the angle of my head during this procedure, with the neck fully extended. Also note the shape of my mouth, expressing grim determination but also pleasure. See, I get a kick out of vaporizing fleas.

A little humor there. Did you get it? I get a kick out of kicking fleas. Ha ha. Pretty clever, huh?

Anyway, that flea thinks he's safe, slipping through the hairs in my armpit, but we'll get him.

Hack, hack, hack!

There! By George, that's one flea we won't see again. When they mess with the Head of Ranch Security, they pay a terrible price.

Now, where were we? I have no idea.

Does anyone remember what we were talking about?

It really burns me up when this happens.

Okay, never mind. We'll start all over. It's me again, Hank the Cowdog. It was early morning, it was summer, it was dry, and it was worse than dry. We were in the second year of a drought, terrible drought. The country looked awful, but oddly enough, the mornings were beautiful—desert mornings with clear, still air and the early sunlight painting our valley with vivid colors of red, orange, and purple.

We had very little grass that summer but a huge population of grasshoppers, and we're talking about those big fat jumbos. Figure that one out. If you have very little grass, how can you have billions of grasshoppers? What do they eat? If grasshoppers don't have grass, how can they hop?

I don't know, but we had billions of them. They not only hopped, but any time I was trotting across the pasture, I could count on getting smacked in the face by four or five of the hateful things. And it hurt.

Nobody on this ranch had anything good to say about grasshoppers, but the wild turkeys were having the time of their lives. They eat grasshoppers, don't you know. Chasing grasshoppers is what they do for a living, so their business was booming.

4

We'll have more to say about turkeys later on.

During this drought, Sally May was trying her best to keep the shrubs and flowers alive in the yard, and she was running the sprinkler in the garden every day to keep the squash, okra, tomatoes, and melons from turning up their toes and dying.

She had succeeded in keeping most of the garden plants alive, and had waged a constant war against the grasshoppers, squash bugs, and tomato worms. Then the deer and rabbits started poaching the green plants. We had a good hog wire fence around the garden, but that didn't stop the rabbits from crawling under it, nor did it keep the deer from jumping over it. In a bad drought, it's hard to keep the poachers out of your garden.

The Security Division had set up a special Task Force to deal with this issue, and let me tell you, we were putting in some hours—day and night, morning and evening, eighteen hours every day, chasing rabbits and deer away from the garden. On this ranch, the work never ends, and in a drought, it neverest enders.

And that's what we were doing on the morning we opened Case #RA-Dash-VS 2335. Loper and Slim had left the ranch before daylight to attend a farm auction. Apparently they thought our ranch didn't have enough junk, so they went shopping for more junk. Sally May was scurrying around the house, trying to get ready for a trip to town. As I recall, she was helping out at Vacation Bible School. Yes, she had volunteered to teach at VBS and this was to be her first day.

Drover and I had slept late. Let me rephrase that. Drover had slept late. I had been up most of the night, doing Poacher Patrol, but the impointant pork is that around seven o'clock in the morning, we were pulling guard duty in Observation Post 9 in front of the machine shed.

All at once, I got a call on the radio. "Hank, you'd better wake up. Something's going on out there."

I leaped to my feet and took command of the ship. "Dive, dive! All ahead two-thirds. Level off at fifty feet and rig for depth charges!" One of the men was standing in front of me. I blinked my eyes and took a closer look. "Who are you?"

"Pretty good. How 'bout yourself?"

"Doing fine, thanks. Are we at fifty feet?"

"Well, I've got four feet and you've got four, and that makes nine."

"Good. Level off at nine feet and let's take a look. Up scope! Who are you and do you have clearance to be here?"

He gazed up at the sky. "Well, I'm Drover. Clarence isn't here."

"Hmmm, that's odd. Do you suppose he went to the engine room?"

"Where's that?"

"Down below, where we keep the engines."

"Down below is where we keep the dirt." He pointed his paw in a downward direction. "That's dirt."

My gaze followed the path indicated by his paw. "Good grief, it IS dirt. We've run aground! Why wasn't I informed? How can I command this ship when nobody tells me...did you say your name is Drover?"

"Yeah, it's me. Hi."

"Hi. Are you the same Drover who was here yesterday?"

"Yep, that's me, Drover with a D."

"Roger that. Okay, bring me up to speed. What's going on around here?"

"Well, I saw some turkeys."

"Rubbish. They must have been seagulls."

"No, they were turkeys."

I melted him with a glare. "Turkeys don't live on the ocean. Get your facts straight."

"We don't have any oceans."

"That's absurd. How can this be a submarine

if we don't have any oceans?"

He moved closer and whispered, "It's not a submarine. It's a ranch in Texas and I think you were dreaming."

I was about to place him under arrest for making slanderous remarks about his commanding officer, but instead, I cut my eyes from side to slide and noticed...hmmm. Everything in my field of vision bore a strong resemblance to...well, a ranch in Texas.

I marched a few steps away and filled my lungs with three big gulps of air. Slowly my head began to clear and I was ready to deal with this latest crisis.

Keep reading. You'll want to hear what happened to the ship.

CHAPTER TWO

A Turkey Alert

I marched over to Drover and gave him a stern glare. "All right, let's go over the details of your report. You said something about seagulls, but if this ranch doesn't have an ocean, they couldn't be seagulls."

"Yeah, they were turkeys."

"Maybe they were turkeys."

"That's what I said."

"Make up your mind and stick with the facts. Why are you rolling your eyes?"

"I don't know. I need some exercise."

"Then why don't you walk or run, jog, jump, or chase a ball? You never DO anything, Drover, except sit on your duff and snap at flies."

"I take naps."

"Yes, and look what it's done to you. Is this why your mother scrimped and saved and sacrificed? So you could become a stub-tailed little hypocardiac who rolls his eyes all the time?"

He grinned. "Good old Mom. I wonder what she's doing today."

"Never mind. Finish your story about the seagulls and quit rolling your eyes. I'm a very busy dog." I began pacing, as I often do when I'm trying to extract information from a rewitless luctant.

A reluctant witness, let us say. I began pacing, while Drover knotted his face into an expression of deep concentration. "Well, let's see. Once upon a time there was a seagull and his name was Sparky, but everyone called him Barky 'cause he had a bad cough, and he lived near the ocean and one day he saw a submarine…"

"Wait. Stop." I paced back over to him. "If you saw turkeys, why are you talking about seagulls?"

"I thought you wanted to hear a story about seagulls."

"I did NOT want to hear a story about seagulls. I'm trying to figure out what's going on around here, and do you know what I think?"

"No, what?"

I moved my mouth closer to his ear. "I think

someone in this department is losing his marbles. Now tell me about the turkeys."

He pointed his left paw toward a flat patch of grass south of the house. "There's seven of 'em."

"Yes, I see the turkeys. Big deal."

Have we discussed wild turkeys? Sally May enjoyed watching them. She put out feed for them and encouraged them to come up close to the house, where she could observe them through her kitchen window. In other words, those turkeys brought joy and pleasure into the life of our Beloved Ranch Wife.

What was so special about watching turkeys? Frankly, I don't get it. My take on turkeys is that they're unusually large birds that spend an unusually large amount of time looking ridiculous. If you ask me, they live hollow, boring little turkey lives, and watching them would be a waste of time.

But that's just a dog's perspectum. Sally May doesn't feel that way. She thinks they're beautiful. That strikes me as a little weird, but I would be the last dog in the world to say a critical word about the Lady of the House. By George, if she enjoys watching the turkeys, our Security Division will do everything in its power to chase them.

Let me rephrase that. The Security Division

will do everything in its power to *protect* them. We protect them from coyotes and cannibals, from raccoons and monsters of the night, and we do it for Sally May.

Back to my conversation with the runt. "Drover, I'm finally seeing a pattern here. They must be turkeys, not seagulls."

"Yeah, and the cat's chasing them."

"What!"

"Look."

I did a quick sweep with field glasses and saw...holy smokes, seven turkeys, and they were being stalked by a cat—a scheming, sulking, spoiled little ranch cat named Pete.

Boy, you talk about righteous anger! I was almost overwhooped by righteous anger, and whirled back to my assistant. "Those birds are being harassed by the local cat. Why wasn't I informed?"

"I tried to tell you."

"Stand by. We're fixing to launch all dogs."

His eyes grew wide and a wicked little grin tugged at the corners of his mouth. "Gosh, you mean..."

"Exactly. We have a free pass to mug the cat. Lock and load, we're going in."

Suddenly the stillness of morning was

shattered by the roar and scream of our P-37 rocket engines, and away we went—down the hill, through that grove of elm trees, past Emerald Pond, and skimming right over the top of the Security Division's Vast Office Complex. Oh, you should have been there to see us!

"Oat Bran, this is Corn Flakes. We are approaching the target. Repeat: we are targeting the approach. Pick an open spot and spot an opening. Let's set these buggies on the ground."

Is this exciting or what? Your ordinary ranch mutts know nothing about this side of life—the danger, the excitement, the roar of the engines, the smell of rocket fumes in the air. Wow, what an adventure.

We landed the aircraft on a level stretch of grass just south of headquarters, leaped out of the pitcocks, and changed into our assault gear. At the same time, I was keeping an eye on Target One, the cat. Pete. Mister Never Sweat. Mister Kitty Moocher. And suddenly I picked up on an interesting detail.

I had launched this mission with the intention of doing some damage to the cat, but what I saw unfolding before my eyes made me have second thoughts. What I saw was a comedy, a display of silliness on a massive scale.

Here's the deal. It appeared that Pete had ventured away from the yard with the idea of playing Leo the Lion, King of the Jungle, and there he was, creeping along on his belly, twitching the last inch of his tail, and stalking the turkeys. After stalking and creeping, he sprang at the birds. That was the funny part. The turkeys just clucked and hopped out of the way.

I mean, they didn't run or fly. They were no more afraid of that cat than they were afraid of a bug, and I could see anger and frustration all over Kitty's face and body. His ears lay flat on his head and the last three inches of his tail were slashing the air, and even at a distance I could hear that unhappy yowl of his, the one that sounds like a police siren.

It's music to a dog's ears. Show me an unhappy cat, and I'll show you a happy dog.

Hee hee. Well, this wasn't what I had expected to find on this mission. It was ten times better. I turned to Drover. "All right, men, stand down."

"Sit down?"

"Stand down."

"Stand up?"

"STAND DOWN!"

He wilted like...I don't know what. Like a weed that had been sprayed with poison, I suppose, and beamed me a Look of Tragedy. "You don't need to yell at me. I hate being yelled at in the morning."

"Well, come back after lunch and we'll try it again."

"It makes me feel like such a failure."

I heaved a sigh and searched for patience. "Drover, what is so difficult about following a simple order?"

"I don't know how to *stand down*. You never explain anything. All you ever do is yell and screech."

"I didn't screech."

"Did too. You screeched right in my left ear."

"Which ear?"

"The right one, and now it's ringing."

"I don't hear any ringing."

"What?"

"I said, I don't hear anything."

He shook his head and stared at the ground. "I can't hear anything. I think you blew out my eardrum."

"I didn't blow out your eardrum, but if it will make you feel better, I'm sorry if I screeched."

His face bloomed into a smile. "No fooling? You're not just saying that?"

"I thought you couldn't hear."

His eyes darted around. "It's better now."

"Oh brother. Are we finished with this?"

"Yeah, but I still don't know how to 'stand down.'"

"All right, let me explain, and please pay attention." There was a long moment of silence. "On second thought, we've run out of time for questions. Let's skip it and move along with our business."

"Oh goodie! We're going to chase the cat?"

"Not so fast. Our mission has changed. Watch this."

Don't leave. You'll want to hear this next part. Hee hee!

CHAPTER THREE

The Invisible Trick

Okay, here's what I did. I turned a big smile toward the cat. "Hey Pete, chasing turkeys this morning? How's that working out for you, huh? Gosh, it's hard to chase turkeys when they don't run."

Boy, you talk about a killer look! Pete's glare was as cold as ice. I gave Drover a wink and a grin. He seemed a little confused at first, then a light came on deep inside the coal mine of his eyes. "Oh, I get it now. Hee hee. We're going to tease the cat?"

"That's correct. Running cats up a tree is good, wholesome entertainment, but taunting them is even better."

"Yeah, and I've heard about taunted houses."

"Absolutely." A silence fell over us. "What did you say?"

"When?"

"Just now. Something about...honking houses?"

"Oh yeah. Well, let me think here." He furrowed his brow and chewed on his lip. "They're full of ghosts."

"No, that's incorrect. *Haunted* houses are full of ghosts. Honking houses are full of geese."

"How come?"

"Because geese honk. Ghosts moan. They don't honk."

"I wonder why."

"I don't know."

"Yeah, but how do all those geese get into the house?"

"If you leave the windows open, geese will fly inside. Once there, they begin honking. Is that clear?"

"Yeah, that helps."

"Good. Quit crossing your eyes."

The cat was coming toward us, so we had to bring this nonsense to an end. I had no idea how we had gotten onto the subject of geese and ghosts. It's the sort of thing that happens when I try to carry on a conversation with Drover.

Sometimes I wonder…

Never mind.

Okay, let's get organized. Pete had been out in the pasture trying to chase turkeys, remember? But he was too fat and slow to catch one, and had succeeded in making himself look ridiculous. And I was loving it.

Here he came, wearing a sour expression and sliding along like the snake he truly was. He greeted me in his usual whiney, annoying tone of voice. "Well, well, it's Hankie the Wonder Dog, and his comical sidekick. What brings you out into the world at such an early hour of the day?"

"The hour might be early to a cat, but we've already put in half a day's work. We're here to investigate a disturbance."

"Oh really. How exciting. Anyone I might know?"

"Yes, as a matter of fact, and let's go straight to the business. Point One, you're bothering Sally May's turkeys. Knock it off. If it happens again, you'll have to deal with the Security Division."

His eyes grew wide. "My goodness! And I guess that means…what? You'll run me up a tree or something?"

"Exactly. Not only will we run you up a tree, but we'll stand at the base of the tree and bark at you for hours and hours."

"Mercy! We don't need that, do we?"

"I thought you'd see it that way."

I shot a wink at Drover. He giggled and whispered, "Boy, you got him on that one. Good shot."

"Thanks, pal. I love this job."

Back to the kitty. He was gazing up at the sky and said, "Let's see, that was Point One. Was there a Point Two?"

"Yes, and I'm glad you asked. Point Two is that you're too fat and lazy to be chasing turkeys. I can't think of a nicer way of saying it." I moved closer and glared into his scheming little eyes. "You looked pathetic, Pete. You got skunked by a bunch of dumb birds. You're an embarrassment to the whole ranch."

"That bad, huh?"

"That bad. Go back to your iris patch and leave the turkey-chasing to those who know how to do it."

He rolled over on his back and began slapping at his tail. "And who might that be, Hankie?"

"The pros, Kitty, coyotes and bobcats. They're in top shape, and they know how to do it. You're not in their league."

"And how about...you?"

"Huh? Me? Well, I..." His question caught me off guard. "I've chased a few turkeys in my time, but that was long ago. I've chosen not to do it any more."

"How noble! Or, could it be," he fluttered his eyelids, "that you've gotten old, fat, and out of shape? That happens, Hankie."

"Yeah? It happens to cats, but not to...will you excuse us a moment? Drover and I need to have a word." I motioned to Drover and we moved a few steps away where we could speak in privacy. "What's this cat up to?"

"You don't reckon he's trying to pull a trick, do you?"

"Of course he is, but the question is, which way is he tricking? See, cats never do the obvious. They feint one way and go the other."

Drover studied the cat. "Well, he hasn't fainted yet, so maybe there's no trick this time."

"Drover, there's always a trick up a cat's sleeve."

"Yeah, but he doesn't have any sleeves."

"That's the whole point. This could be the old Invisible Trick trick. I've seen it before."

"If it's invisible, how can you see it?"

"What?"

"I said...what'll we do now?"

I threw a glance over to the cat. He was rolling around in the grass and playing with his tail. "Okay, listen up. Our response will come in two stages. In Stage One, we will play dumb."

"That rhymes. Stage One, play dumb."

"Never mind that it rhymes."

"That rhymes too."

"Drover, please concentrate. Repeat our orders for Stage One."

He wadded up his face and squinted one eye. "Let's see. We honk?"

The air hissed out of my lungs. "No, we don't honk. We play dumb."

"Boy, that'll be hard."

"I know, but we have to pull it off. In Stage One, we want Kitty to think we're just a couple of dumb dogs."

"Got it. What about Stage Three?"

I struggled to control my temper. "We don't have a Stage Three."

"Oh, sorry. What about Stage Four?"

"Stage Four will be complicated, so pay attention. We will expose his Invisible Trick. We'll figure out what he doesn't want us to do, then we won't do the opposite. We'll chop down the trees until we find the forest, and please don't roll your eyes when I'm giving instructions."

"Sorry, but I'm confused."

"Here's all you need to know." I tapped myself on the head. "I've got it all right here. Just follow my lead. Any questions?"

"How come we're doing all this stuff?"

I lifted my head to a proud angle and looked him straight in the eyes. "We're doing it because he's a cat and we're dogs. It's our doggie as dudes to keep the cats humble. You're rolling your eyes again."

"I didn't understand what you just said."

"It's our duty as dogs to keep the cats humble. That's what this life is all about."

"I'll be derned."

"Are we ready? Break!"

We broke the huddle and returned to Sally May's rotten little cat, the same one who thought he was smart enough to trick the entire Security Division. Ha. Little did he know. This time, we had the little sneak exactly where he wanted us.

I marched over to him. "Okay, Pete, the Ranch Council wants an explanation of that last remark you made."

"Oh really. Which one was that?"

"Your suggestion that I might be too old or lazy to chase turkeys."

"Oh, that one!"

"Did you say that in hopes of provoking me into chasing the turkeys? In other words, was this another of your slimy tricks? And don't forget that you're under oath."

"Well, just darn the luck. How can I lie, cheat, and steal if I'm under oath?"

"You can't."

"So...you're saying that I have to tell the truth?"

"That's correct, and the Council is waiting to hear your answer."

He rolled over on his belly and began clawing the grass. "Well, Hankie, you've got me backed into a corner, and if I must tell the truth, here it is." He widened his eyes and spoke in a creepy tone of voice. "Of course I was hoping to trick you into chasing the turkeys. What else would you expect a cat to do?"

Drover and I exchanged glances. "The Council will take a two minute recess. Don't leave, Kitty." I jerked my head at Drover and we went back to Chambers for a conference.

You're probably aching to know what we said in Chambers. Sorry, but these conferences are highly classified and nobody gets into the room without going through Security. If you don't flash the right badge, you don't get in, period. Sorry.

Oh, what the heck, maybe it wouldn't hurt to let you in, but you have to promise not to blab this around, okay?

Here we go.

I Fool the Cat,
Hee Hee

I brought the meeting to order, and Drover was the first to speak. "What do we do when a cat tells the truth?"

I tried not to laugh. "Don't you get it? He's telling the truth to *conceal* the truth. It's typical cat behavior. His greatest fear is that we might chase the turkeys and do it right."

"Who's we?"

I placed a paw on his shoulder. "That's the best part of our plan. You see, his plot called for *me* to chase the turkeys. He never dreamed that we might switch agents and send you into combat. This will blow his trick to smithereens."

Drover's eyes blanked out.

"What's wrong?"

"Well, this old leg's been acting up."

"Exercise will do it a world of good."

"By dose is stobbed ub."

"Fresh air will fix that. Are you ready?"

"Help!"

He tried to run, but I blocked his path. "This is your big moment, soldier." I pointed to the turkeys, who were still standing nearby and watching us. "There they are. Run through the middle of them. And remember: this isn't about you or me. We're doing it for dogs all over the world. What do you say?"

My words seemed to have a magic effect on him. The little mutt puffed himself up to his full height. To be honest, he wasn't all that tall, but he did his best and squeezed up every inch of height out of his backbone. And in a voice that shocked me with its tone of authority, he said, "So this is for dogs all over the world?"

"Absolutely."

"It's not just about me?"

"No, no. This is bigger than both of us, son."

"I think I can do it!"

I was so proud, tears sprang to my eyes. After years of being a weenie, my assistant had finally decided to become a hot dog. He leaped to his feet, I mean like a lion or a tiger, and turned a flaming gaze toward the circus of turkles...the circle of turkeys, let us say.

Trying to hold back the flood of emotion, I yelled, "Go get 'em, soldier! Show the cat what dogs are really made of!"

And off he went like a...

Huh?

Oh brother! I take back everything I said about Drover. Mark out those lines in your book. No, better yet, cut them out with scissors and burn the pieces.

Do you know what he did? He took off like a guided mistletoe and headed for the turkeys, then hooked a ninety-degree turn to the left and highballed it straight to the machine shed—while I was cheering him on to victory and wiping tears of joy out of my eyes!

Oh, the treachery! It almost broke my heart.

I was so shocked, I could hardly speak, but at last I was able to yell, "Drover, return to base at once, and that is a direct order!" He kept going, didn't even look back. "Drover, you will be court-martialed for this! You will stand in the corner until your nose drops off, and then we will feed it to the buzzards!"

He was gone, ZOOM, into the darkness of his Secret Sanctuary.

I should have known. See, I'm too soft-hearted, too easy on the men. When you've got a jughead like Drover in the ranks, you have to stay on him all the time. You can't let up for a second, because if you do, he'll do just what he did.

Well, getting sandbagged by Drover was bad enough, but I had to prepare myself for something even worse. This shameless act of treason had taken place RIGHT IN FRONT OF MY WORST ENEMY, exposing all the cracks and flaws in the upper ranks of the Security Division. Now he would think that we were an undisciplined mob of ninnies, and the very thought of what he might do with that information sent chills down my backbone.

I couldn't bring myself to look at the little pestilence, but I lifted my Earatory Scanners and began probing the air waves for the sounds of him laughing his head off. To my shock and amazement, I heard nothing. Slowly I turned my eyes in his direction, and here's what I saw.

He was sitting now, with his tail tucked around his back side and his front feet together. He was gazing off into the distance...and he wasn't laughing. He wasn't even smiling.

Well, this defied the rules of logic and the laws

of physics. There was something very fishy going on here, and I had to get to the bottom of the pond. Salvaging what was left of my dignity, I marched over to him.

"Okay, Pete, out with it."

"What ever do you mean, Hankie?"

"You ought to be enjoying this moment. You ought to be laughing, but you're just sitting there like an...I don't know, like a piece of furniture."

His gaze drifted around to me. "It has to do with the game, Hankie. It's no fun when the game is too easy." He heaved a heavy sigh. "I always win, and to be perfectly frank, it's gotten boring."

My ears jumped. "Wait just a second, pal. I might have lost, but you didn't win. We were on to your Invisible Trick and that's why we switched from me to Drover as the turkey-chaser. That was MY idea. The only problem was that Drover chickened out."

He shrugged. "Hankie, you did exactly what I wanted you to do. I had it planned that way from the beginning. I won, and it's so depressing, I'm going to give it up."

A deep silence throbbed between us. "Give up what?"

"This endless game of dogs and cats, Hankie,

the never-ending battle of tricks and counter-tricks."

I couldn't believe what I'd just heard. "No kidding? You're quitting?" He nodded and I burst out laughing. "Well, by George, it took a few years, but we've finally worn out the enemy! That's not the sweetest kind of victory, but I guess we'll take it. See you around, sucker."

"Pretty soon, I'll wager."

Holy smokes, I had finally defeated the cat and won the National Championship! I marched away from the little fraud, and it was one of the finest moments of my entire career. Not only had I crushed the cat, but in doing so, I had proven, once and for all, that discipline, endurance, persistence, and righteousness will win every...

Wait a second. I stopped in my tracks. All at once, I heard two voices inside my head. One was yelling, "We're number one! We're number one!" The other was whispering, "No more game means...NO MORE GAME."

You will find this next part shocking. All of a sudden, my feet were, uh, taking me back, more or less in the general direction of the cat, and I found myself...well, standing beside him.

"Pete? You got a minute? We need to talk."

He swiveled his head around and stared at

me. "We just talked, Hankie."

"That's what we need to talk about."

"We need to talk about what we talked about? Hmmm. This sounds mysterious."

"It's not mysterious, you little...can we go straight to the bottom line?"

He thought about that. "Yes, let's do."

"You can't quit the game."

"Oh really? Why is that, Hankie?"

"Because...look, Pete, I don't know how to say this except to say it. Quitting the game is just wrong, it's unnatural."

"I know, Hankie, but it's become so boring and predictable, I can't go on with it."

"Okay, I've got an idea. Hear me out." I began pacing a circle around the little...around the cat, let us say, and I must admit that my mind was in a swirl. "Pete, these little games are...this is hard for me to say...they're probably more important to me than I'd like to admit."

"Oh really."

"Yes. In small but tiny ways, they seem to contribute to my..."

"Your enjoyment of life?"

"Right."

"Your sense of dogness?"

"Perfect, yes, my sense of dogness. You nailed

it. Okay, you're bored with the game because you win all the time, right? Isn't that what you said?"

He nodded and licked his left front paw. "That's what I said. Go on."

"Here's an idea. We'll start the game all over again—a new game, Pete, a fresh start—only this time, *I'll win*."

His eyes lit up. "My, my, what an interesting idea! I wouldn't have thought of that. It *would* freshen things up and bring some variety into the game, wouldn't it?"

"Right. I think it would, Pete." I paced over to him. "We'll go back to the turkey business, see, but this time without tricks and counter-tricks. Everything's up front and on the table. All you have to do is make it clear what's *really and truly* in your heart: Would you rather that I chased the turkeys or didn't chase them?"

He stared at me with his weird cattish eyes. "And you're saying that I have to tell the truth?"

"That's correct. You have to be up-front and honest. Otherwise…well, it would be just another slimy trick."

He made a sputtering sound, probably a cough. "Very well, Hankie, let's give it a try. Now, let's see if I've got it straight. I'll pick the outcome that I really and truly want, and you'll do the opposite?"

"Exactly. I'll win, you'll lose, and the game stays fresh and exciting."

"Hankie, this is the work of a genius."

"Thanks, pal. I hate to keep saying this, but there's a reason why they made me Head of Ranch Security. Okay, choose your outcome."

He rolled his eyes up to the sky. "Very well, Hankie. In my deepest, most secret heart of hearts, I hope you DON'T chase the turkeys."

"You're being sincere about this?"

"Oh yes! It would upset me terribly if you happened to catch one."

I reached out a paw and gave the little guy a pat on the back. "Okay, Pete, it's a new day and a new game. I think this is going to work."

"Oh, I hope so, Hankie. I'll kee-hee keep an open mind."

"Let the game begin. Watch this."

Can you believe the little dummy fell for this? I had tricked him into exposing his Invisible Trick, see, and now all I had to do was...it was a little confusing, to be honest, but I was on track to deliver the little sneak the most shattering defeat of his life.

Have you ever seen a top-of-the-line, blue

ribbon cowdog run through a bunch of turkeys? Wow. I crammed the throttle all the way up to Turbo Six, and you talk about fireworks and feathers! I plowed 'em.

"Hank, leave the turkeys alone!"

I chased and barked, barked and chased, plowed through the middle of them, did a one-eighty, and made another pass.

"Get away from my turkeys, you hound!"

Birds hopped and flew in all directions, and one of them happened to be slow and careless, heh heh, so I put a bite on his tail section.

"Hank, if I ever get my hands on you..."

I snagged him and, well, he began thrashing my nose with his wings. Ouch. It hurt like crazy but I held on for dear life, and happened to turn my head to the north and saw...

Huh?

Sally May?

Oops

WHERE DID SHE COME FROM?

She hadn't been anywhere in sight when we'd started this deal, but she was in sight now, and storming straight towards me.

Have we mentioned that when she's in a bad mood, you can see it in her manner of walking? It's true. She has what we call The Walk of Anger. She leans forward at the waist, swings her arms, and sets her feet down hard on every step. You'd almost describe it as "stomping," only ladies don't stomp, right? Oh, and the expression on her face was a little scary.

That's what I was seeing, and to be honest, it made me uneasy. I released the turkey from the grip of my grapple, and hurried over to the cat.

"Pete, we've got a problem. Do you see who's coming this way?" He nodded. "She looks mad, doesn't she?" He nodded. "I think I'm in trouble." He nodded. "This wasn't part of our plan. I never thought..."

There was something about the way he looked at me in that moment. It wasn't much, just a tiny curl of the mouth and the cut of his eyes, but it caused the rafters to start falling in the attic of my mind. "Wait a second!"

He fluttered his eyelids and whispered, "Congratulations, you won. Well, I'd better be going. You and Sally May have things to discuss."

And with that, the little sneak...the little liar...the little cheater went scampering back to the yard, leaving me with...oh brother.

Do you see the meaning of this? I hope you don't. It's so embarrassing, I don't want to talk about it, but there's no way we can avoid it. Sally May arrived on the scene, and boy, was she mad.

I knew what was coming and began preparing for the storm, flipping switches in the control room of my mind. I activated the Emergency Remorse Program which gave us Sad Eyes, Dead Tail, and Ears With No Hope. Are you familiar with ERP? The software actually changes the shape of the body, don't you see, and bends the spinal region into the shape of an arc, with the head hanging down in front and the tail dragging the ground on the back side.

It's a dandy program and we save it back for extreme emergencies. This appeared to be one of those. I mean, the woman was seriously angry.

I had just activated ERP when she arrived. She towered over me and parked her hands on her hips, always a bad sign. Her eyes blazed with unholy light, her nostrils were flared, and her lips were forming words I couldn't hear.

At last she spoke. "How many times do I have to tell you? DON'T CHASE MY TURKEYS!"

Yes, but...

"I want them to come up around the house."

Right, but Pete...

"I want them to feel welcome. What's wrong with you?"

Well, I...

"You are so dumb!"

Ouch.

Hey, her rotten little cat...it was complicated, and there was no way I could explain it with looks and wags. I could only hope that the Remorse Program would do its job and get me out of this mess.

She shook her head, muttered, stared off into the distance, shifted her weight from one leg to the other, and brushed a wisp of hair away from her forehead. The seconds crept by and slowly the ice in her face began to melt. When she spoke again, she seemed close to tears.

"I'm turning into a wicked witch. I hate being this way. I don't want to spend my whole life yelling at the dogs, but Hank..." She sat down in the grass beside me and looked into my eyes. "Look, if you will just do as you're told, we can get along. I don't expect you to be a saint, but I have rules. You're a dog and you have to follow my rules."

I didn't know where this was going, but we appeared to be making progress. I went to Cautious Taps on the tail section.

She continued. "The rules are simple. Don't chase my turkeys. Don't scatter my chickens. Stay out of the sewer. Don't bark all night. Stay out of my yard. Don't dig in the garden. Stop tormenting my cat. Does any of that seem unreasonable?"

Uh...well, I'd been with her right up to the business about "tormenting" her cat, and that one...she had no idea! He was Mister Kitty Perfect while she was around, but the minute she went into the house…she just didn't know.

I increased the speed and sincerity of my wags and beamed her a message: "Sally May, we have a few differences of opinion, but I think we can work this out. No kidding. There's nothing I want more than to patch up our relationship."

She looked up at the sky. "We have so much to be thankful for—our family, our home, good health, this ranch. We're blessed beyond measure. Nobody on this place should ever spend a single day being unhappy, and I should never be…" her voice trembled, "…screaming at the dogs."

Great point.

She heaved a sigh and fixed her gaze on me. "Come here, you poor, disobedient, misunderstood bonehead of a dog."

I wasn't sure exactly what she meant by that, but she'd said it in a gentle voice, so I dared to move a few steps closer. She extended her hand.

"Oh, I'm not going to bite your head off. Come here and I'll pet you, but don't you dare lick me on the face."

Oops, that's exactly what I'd planned to do, so it was a good thing she'd given me the heads-up. With Sally May, we have to suppress Licks on the Face and Licks on the Ankles.

I moved another step closer and she swept me

into her arms. I was amazed. She pulled me into a hug, and we're talking about a firm embrace with her cheek pressing against the top of my head.

"Oh, you smell awful!"

It was one of the tenderest moments we'd ever experienced.

"I'm sorry I lost my temper and screeched and turned into an old hag. But Hank, please, stop chasing my turkeys, okay?"

Was this touching or what? This was the moment we'd been hoping for and working towards, the event that would turn our relationship around. Yes, we could do it! I would take a pledge never to chase the turkeys again...unless her scheming little cat...no, I couldn't go on blaming the stupid cat for all my problems.

This was MY LIFE, by George, and from this day forward...

I don't know how this happened. Actually, I do know how it happened, and it was an incredible piece of bad luck. See, just as we had reached this precious moment in our relationship, a fly landed on my right ear and began drilling. I went to Ear Flicks, hoping to dislodge the little heathen, but he kept drilling. It hurt, and we're talking about a serious, big-time hurt.

So what's a dog supposed to do? I jerked my head upwards with a mighty heave and...I'm not sure I can go on with this, I mean, it was dreadful.

Could we talk about something else? I just can't bring myself...sigh. We might as well get it over with.

Okay, I gave my head a mighty upward jerk, don't you see, and...well, the top of my head hit her on the face. Hard. Below the left eye.

Oops.

For a long moment, we were enveloped in a deadly, choking silence. Her hand moved to her eye and felt around.

At last she spoke. "If you gave me a black eye..." She scrambled to her feet, bent at the waist, and brought her face right down to mine. Hmm. The skin below her eye seemed to be turning blue. *I have to teach Vacation Bible School this morning!*"

She whirled around and headed back to the house in a rapid walk. She hadn't gone more than, oh, fifty steps, when she stopped and looked back at me. "Idiot! Leave my turkeys alone!" She stormed away and didn't look back, but I heard what she said. "I hope you're happy!"

Well, I wasn't happy. I felt terrible. I mean, you talk about lousy luck! We'd been so close to patching things up. We'd hugged and bonded and everything. She'd apologized for screeching at me and saying hateful things, and now she was back to screeching and saying hateful things. It appeared that our relationship had fallen back into ruins.

And the saddest part was that it had all been caused by one measly fly—one measly fly and a certain slithery, slimy, little creep of a cat. Could I blame Pete for a fly that had drilled a hole in my ear and caused my head to leap up and collide with Sally May's cheek? Of course I could! If he hadn't actually caused it, he wished that he had caused it, and that was close enough.

You know, dogs bring a very important perspective on world history. All those wars and famines and riots we hear about? Dig deep and guess what you'll find at the bottom of it. A CAT. Cats have caused 97% of all the misery and turmoil in the...

I couldn't figure out how the little snot had lured me into chasing the turkeys. *I did not understand it*. It left me speechless. See, I'd known that Pete and I were engaged in a deadly game of chess. I'd been alert to his tricks, on my guard, watching his every move and gesture. And still, I got rolled!

You know, it takes a great deal of courage to defend the position that cats are stupid. When they keep winning, it really messes up the argument, but I will continue to...phooey. He makes me sick.

The point to take home from all this is that, in certain mysterious ways, Pete had injured Sally May's face, and that's all we need to know. I don't want to talk about it any more.

Which brings us to another dreary subject: Drover. He would get a fair and balanced trial, but we already knew the outcome. He needed a jailhouse, is what he needed, and I was just the dog to give it to him.

I took an indirect route to the machine shed. I had no reason to suppose that my presence near the house and yard would cause eruptions of joy, shall we say, so I made a wide loop out into the horse pasture and came in from the west. I was walking along, preparing myself for the upcoming trial, when, suddenly, I found myself standing nose to nose with a cow—a red cow with big horns and an orange tag in her left ear, bearing the number 35.

Those details will become very important later on, but somehow they didn't register in my memory banks. I was busy, on my way to court, and in no mood to deal with cattle issues, so I gave her a bark. "Out of the way, you old bat!"

That might have been the wrong approach. She dropped her head, snorted like a buffalo, pawed the ground, and came a-hooking. I won't go into all the details, but it was a close call and a near-miss. I managed to escape, but it was a little tense there for a while.

Then I resumed my march to the court house...and suddenly it hit me like a goose falling out of the sky: red cow, horns, tag #35. *That was the Phantom Cow*! I had just come face to face with...hang on, we need to stop right here and pull up her file.

See, I'd had some dealings with this cow, and she wasn't normal. Normal cows are herd animals. They stay with the bunch. The Phantom Cow stayed off by herself and lived a solitary life, I mean like a hermit. During the day, she hid out in the brush along the creek or stayed up in the canyons north of headquarters, and came out at night to graze. That is normal behavior for a deer. It's not normal for a cow.

For months at a time, nobody saw her and we never knew where she might turn up. A barbed wire fence meant nothing to her and she went wherever she wanted. She didn't even come in to feed in the wintertime, which tells you just how weird she was, because cattle are gluttons in the wintertime. Show them a sack of free food and they'll run over you to steal a bite.

The Phantom Cow dined alone, lived alone, hated people and dogs, and stay away from civilization...yet I had just caught her hanging around ranch headquarters. What was the deal? It was a dark, disturbing mystery that eventually led me into...

We don't have time to go into it right now. Don't forget, I was on my way to Drover's court martial, but keep the Phantom Cow in mind. She will return like a bad dream, and when she does, you will be scared into next week. Honest.

Drover's
Court Martial

Where were we? Oh yes, Drover's court martial.

I crept up to the big sliding doors on the front of the machine shed and was about to shout the order for him to come out with his paws in the air, when I thought I heard a sound coming from inside. I cocked my ears and listened. Yes, it was a sound, all right, and unless I was badly mistaken, somebody was in there...singing?

Well, this promised to send the case in an entirely different direction. Drover wasn't exactly famous for his singing, but who else could it be? My mind flashed over a list of possible suspects: Eddy the Rac, the coyote brotherhood, Wallace and Junior? Nothing matched up, so I crept through the crack between the sliding doors, cranked up Earatory Scanners, and monitored the situation.

Here's what I heard. You won't believe this. Roll tape.

Joe Fred, The Grasshopper

The grasshopper said,
"They call me Joe Fred.
If you bring me some breakfast, I'll get out of bed."

Then Joe Freddie hopped
And said he could not
Hope to hop farther before he got stopped.

Sing hickory dickery dockery doe.
I'll tie a red ribbon around your big toe.
Sing hickory snickory snockery snook.
Joe went back to bed and opened a book.

The grasshopper said
As he laid in his bed,
"Reading is fun but I need to be fed."

He murmured a sigh,
"Please bring me some pie.

Without it, I fear that I surely will die."

Sing hickory dickery dockery doze.
I'll tie a red ribbon around your big nose.
Sing hickory slickory slockery silk.
He washed down the pie with a pitcher of milk.

He ate like a pig,
His tummy was big,
He fell out of bed and sat on a twig.

He turned his head round
And heard a big sound.
The twig broke in half and he fell to the ground.

Sing hickory dickery dockery deer.
I'll tie a red ribbon around your left ear.
Sing hickory slickory slockery sled.
Joe Fred was exhausted and went back to bed.

And now I will quit, 'cause that's all of the song.

Oh brother. What a piece of musical junk! By now, you've probably figured out who was responsible for it. Drover, who else?

I'd heard enough. "All right, Drover, you can come out now. We've put the entire building under lockdown."

There was a moment of silence, then I heard his voice coming from the backest, farrest, darkest corner. "How'd you know I was in here?"

"I heard you singing."

"Oh drat, I didn't think about that. Did you like my song?"

"Come out and we'll discuss it."

"Oh, I'd rather stay here."

"Out! Now!"

He took his sweet time, but finally he emerged from the shadows—walking at the speed of a turtle, gazing around, and wearing his patented silly grin. "Oh, hi. Here I am."

"Congratulations. I won't bother to read you your rights."

"Thanks."

"You don't have any."

"What does that mean?"

"You're under arrest."

His eyes popped wide open. "Arrest? Gosh, what did I do?"

"That will be the subject of your court martial, and we might as well get right to it. Sit down, make yourself comfortable." He sat down and I began pacing circles around him. "How do you plead?"

"Oh, red, I guess."

"Explain that."

"Well, my blood is red."

"Good for you. So what?"

"Well, when I bleed, it's mostly red."

I marched over to him and leaned into his face. "I said plead. *P-p-p-plead!*"

He flinched and blinked his eyes. "You sprayed me in the face."

"Sorry, but when you don't listen, I have to exaggerate my words." I resumed my pacing. "Let's try this again. How do you plead? And red is not an option. Innocent or guilty?"

He rolled his eyes around. "Well, I feel guilty a lot of the time. It just eats me up."

"Tell this court about your feelings of guilt."

"Well, let's see. I've always tried to be a good little doggie. I promised Mom that I would be, but sometimes...I just feel like a rat."

"Ah, now we're getting somewhere, and already I've found a fly in your ornament. Look at your tail and tell this court what you see."

He twisted around and...oh brother, he fell over backwards. "I can't see it."

"Yes, but deep in your cheating little heart, you know what's there, don't you?"

He lowered his head and began to sniffle.

"Yeah, but I don't want to talk about it."

"You have no choice. Sit up straight and tell this court what your tail would look like if you could see it."

He picked himself up and returned to the witness chair. "If I could see my tail, it would be long, and that's what I've always wished for, but I can't see it 'cause it's so short. For as long as I can remember," his voice quivered, "I've had a stub tail."

"Exactly my point. Don't try to convince this court that you feel like a rat. You can't possibly feel like a rat, *because your tail is too short!*"

Wow, what a bolt of lighting. The little mutt was stunned and finally whimpered, "Can I leave now?"

"No. We're just getting started. Having destroyed your claim that you've felt like a rat all your life, I will now read the list of charges." I glanced down at my yellow legal pad and read the long list. "Insubordination, treason, treachery, disobedience, desertion, failure to render aid, cowardice in front of a cat, and cheating. What do you have to say for yourself?"

"I left 'cause I knew it was another one of Pete's tricks."

"So! You *knew* and didn't tell your commanding

officer? Is that what you're saying?"

"Yeah, 'cause you never listen."

"Guilty as charged!" I walked over to him and glared into his eyeballs. "Soldier, we've got enough dirt to put you away for a hundred years, but I'm feeling generous. This court sentences you to one hour with your nose in the corner. To the brig, march!"

We'd been through this routine so many times, I didn't have to tell him which corner in which to put his nose into which. He went straight to the southeast corner and stood in the Nose Position.

The worst part of this deal was that I had to stand guard. I didn't dare leave him, see, because I knew he would cheat. The little goof had spent so much time around the cat, we couldn't trust him to follow the Code of Honor.

I paced and yawned, scratched a few fleas, and time sure did crawl. After what seemed hours, he broke the silence. "What did you think of the song? I wrote it myself."

"Do you want my honest opinion?"

"No, just tell me it was great."

"It wasn't great. It wasn't even good. It was the worst piece of musical junk I've ever heard. Why would you make up a song about a grasshopper?"

"Well, we've got a lot of 'em this year. There's no sense in letting 'em go to waste."

"Drover, everyone hates grasshoppers. Grasshoppers have no friends, and nobody wants to hear a song about one."

"Yeah, but he had a name: Joe Fred. I thought that was pretty neat."

"It wasn't neat, it was ridiculous. And you know what else? If you keep talking about it, you might get court-martialed again for writing tiresome little songs."

"Can I get out of prison now?"

"Absolutely not."

"Maybe we can make a deal."

"I don't make deals with prisoners."

"I found a nest."

"You're wasting my time, Drover."

"There were three eggs in it, and I didn't eat 'em."

"I care nothing about...what kind of eggs?"

"Chicken eggs, I guess."

"Why didn't you eat them?"

"Well, they had shells."

"All eggs have shells. They're called 'egg shells.'"

"Yeah, but what about shotguns?"

"Shotguns have shells too, but the point is..."

I paced over to him. "Drover, bribing a guard is a very serious…you said three eggs?"

"Yep."

"Any bacon?"

"Nope, just eggs, and they looked pretty good."

"Hmm." I examined all the clues under the microscope of my mind. "Maybe we'd better check it out."

"Can I get out of jail?"

"If there is actually a nest, and if it actually contains three eggs, we might suspend your sentence."

He leaped with joy. "Oh goodie! Follow me." And with that, he went scampering into the dark and gloomy depths of the machine shed.

You'll never guess what we found back there.

CHAPTER SEVEN

Poisoned

Here we go. I followed Drover into the dark and spooky part of his Secret Sanctuary. Near the northwest corner, where Loper kept his canoe and Sally May kept her grandmother's furniture, we found a crude nest in the dust.

The nest contained three eggs. Are you surprised? You should be, for the simple reason that Drover's tips usually turn out to be wrong. Somehow this one turned out to be correct.

You're probably wondering why a hen would lay eggs in a barn when she could do it a lot easier in the chicken house. Great question. I mean, Sally May had fixed up her chicken house into a five-star hotel for birds. It had everything a hen could want, including two rows of straw-lined nests.

The answer lies in the psychobirdicle makeup of a chicken's mind, and there's a nice, big scientific word you might want to add to your vocabinetry list. Let's take a closer look at this interesting word and break it down into parts.

Psycho-bird-icle. "Psycho" means crazy, "bird" means chicken, and "icle" means...I'm not sure what it means, but it shows up in other words, such as icicle and bicycle. Perhaps we place "icle" on the end of a long word to equalize the weight, so that it doesn't tip over and fall out of the sentence. But the important thing is that when we put all three pieces together, we get a nice, big word that means "crazy chicken icle."

And now we understand why a hen might lay eggs outside the chicken house—because your average chicken is dumb beyond belief. If you take that as your starting point, it's perfectly reasonable that a chicken would walk past a five-star chicken-house hotel and lay a bunch of eggs in a dusty barn.

How do I know so much about chickens? I live with the morons. I watch them all the time. I get paid to protect them from bad guys who love chicken dinners. Slurp. Please disregard that sound. It meant almost nothing.

I know chickens, is the point, and they're liable to squat down and lay an egg anywhere on the ranch. And you know what else? Half the time, they go off chasing bugs and forget where they laid the eggs. Unbelievable. They are dumb beyond dumb.

Anyways, some disoriented hen had left a bonanza of eggs for me in the machine shed, so let's rush on with the mush. Mush on with the story, that is.

Drover was excited. "There it is. Are you proud of me?"

I pushed him aside and began collecting evidence. A Sniffatory Analysis confirmed that they were indeed chicken eggs, which was an important piece of information. Do you know why? Buzzards have been known to lay eggs in barns, and nobody wants to eat a buzzard omelet.

Drover was watching and drooling. "What are you going to do with 'em?"

"Well, I'm not going to hatch them out. We can start there."

"Are you going to eat 'em?"

"That's correct. Eggs laid outside the chicken house are fair game, and Sally May will never miss them."

His eyes blazed with gluttony. "Gosh, maybe I

could eat one."

I stuck my nose in his face. "You will *not* eat one. They're mine. Your reward is a free pass from jail. Now scram, go scratch a flea."

"Well, you don't need to get all hateful about it."

"Sorry, I've had a bad day."

"Yeah, I watched. Hee hee."

I melted him with a glare. "You'd better leave or you might end up spending the rest of your life behind bars. Scram!"

At last he left, but he'd gotten one thing right. (A little humor there, did you get it? He *left* but got one thing *right*. Ha ha.). Anyways, he got one thing right: Pete had really ambushed me on that turkey deal, and I made a mental note to add his name to my Doom List.

I waited until Drover had slipped through the crack between the sliding doors, then turned my attention to the feast that lay before me: three nice, big, fresh country eggs that were just waiting for a dog to give them a slurp...to give them a home.

My eyes were smoldering with Omelet Desire. My tongue had to work a double shift to keep the water mopped up inside my mouth. I took one last glance over both shoulders, just to be absolutely sure that Radar Woman wasn't lurking in the shadows.

Then and only then did I lower my nose to ground level, scoop the first of the eggs into my mouth, and crunch down. The shell made a pleasant crackling sound and my mouth tingled with...my mouth tingled with...

You know, it had kind of a cheesy taste, and that seemed odd. Oh well, omelets often contain cheese and dogs love omelets, so...no problem. I gulped it down and spit out the shells. It was then that I noticed...

Green? The inside of the shells was green and the air seemed to contain the odor of...was that sulfur?

Huh?

I cut my eyes from side to side. Remember our discussion about chickens laying eggs all over the ranch and forgetting where they left them? Guess what happens in the summertime to the eggs that don't get hatched. They become ROTTEN EGGS. They turn green inside and reek of sulfur and...*holy cow, I had just eaten one!*

I needed some air, fast. I sprinted to the door and staggered outside. There, I grabbed a big gulp of air and...found myself looking straight into the eyes of Drover. He seemed despondent.

"Oh hi. How were the eggs?"

"I only ate one."

A sparkle came into his eyes. "You left two for me? Oh boy! Thanks a bunch!"

"Wait. Drover..."

Too late, he was gone. For a moment, I thought of rushing back inside to warn him, but then...no, by George, let him learn a valuable lesson about gluttony. Experience is the best teacher, right? That very morning, I had learned a powerful lesson about the treachery of cats, and he might as well get some schooling on eggs. Hee hee.

Sorry, I shouldn't laugh. It might be constroodled as heartless and mean, but you have to admit it was pretty funny.

It didn't take long for the little mutt to go to school on rotten eggs. Within seconds, I heard a scream inside the barn, and moments later he emerged, looking as though he'd just swallowed a spider.

I tried to put on a serious face. "Drover, you have green foam all over your mouth, and you're looking pale."

He gasped for air. "What were those things?"

"Well, they were rotten eggs. If you hadn't been such a greedy pig, I would have told you not to eat them."

"Yeah, but I did eat 'em! Help, murder, I'm going to be sick, oh, my leg!"

In spite of his so-called bad leg, he made a dash down to the corrals and dived into the stock tank. For the next three minutes, he dog-paddled around the tank and gargled water to get the taste out of his mouth. Then he staggered out of the tank and proceeded to throw up his toenails, and we're talking about all over the corrals.

The place would be contaminated for months.

It was a sad spectacle. Hee hee. Okay, it was pretty funny.

Well, to quote a wise old saying, his eggs had come home to roost. Greed hath its price, and so does Attempted Bribery. Don't forget that he had bribed his way out of jail, only to fall victim to his own vanilla. His own villainy, let us say. It was kind of inspiring, the way his deeds had come back to honk him, and it confirmed that justice will always...

Borp.

Excuse me. It confirmed that justice will always...you know, my stomach was a little uneasy, come to think of it, but let me point out that I didn't get sick and barf all over the ranch. Do you know why? Some dogs are tough, and some dogs are little weenies. Little weenie dogs

68

have little weenie stomachs, and they get sick over nothing.

Take your average poodle as an example. Just say "rotten egg" to a poodle and he'll go into convulsions. They'll have to rush him to the vet clinic and pump out his stomach and put him on bupp. Excuse me. On medication.

Drover wasn't a poodle, but sometimes he acted like one, and I can tell you that at several staff meetings, his weenie ways had been a major topic of discussion. There was even talk of firing him.

This latest incident with the eggs wouldn't do him any good with the Chief Joints of Stuff. The Jointed Chiefs of...borp. Excuse me. The Joint Chiefs of Staff. Unless Drover took steps to toughen up, his future with the Security Division was going to be a matter of concern.

I don't want to sound cold-hearted. I knew the little mutt tried to be strong, but his behavior reflected badly on the whole organization. How did it make us look when one of our employees spent half an hour, gargling water in a stock tank and throwing up all over the ranch? Bad. It stained the reputation of the entire Security Division.

Oh well. He would either toughen up or

continue his weenie ways, and there wasn't a thing I could do about it. I was lost in these thoughts when, all at once and out of nowhere, I heard a voice in the distance.

I lifted Earatory Scanners and began pulling in sound waves. There it was again, the voice of a child. Unless I was badly mistaken, he was calling...us, his dogs.

"Here Hankie! Here Drover! Here doggies!"

By that time, Drover had dragged himself back up the hill and was looking...well, not so good. "Drover, we've been summoned."

"I'm sick."

"Little Alfred wants us to report to the yard gate at once."

"Why didn't you tell me those eggs were rotten?"

"First, you were in such a rush to make a hog of yourself, I didn't have a chance to warn you. Second, you needed to learn Life's Lessons on your own. And third, you watched me get sandbagged by the cat and said 'hee hee'."

"Well, I'm not saying 'hee hee' now."

"Good. We're making progress."

He gave me a mournful look. "How come you didn't get sick?"

"Self-borp...self-discipline. Tell yourself you

won't get sick and you won't get sick. Mind over matter. Are you going on this mission or not?"

"I'm out. I'd have to feel better to die."

"Very well, but this will go into my report."

I left him there and sprinted down the hill. There, I found…you'll see.

Anything For the Kids

The boy was standing beside his mother's car which was parked behind the house, beside the yard gate. As I drew closer, I did a Visual Sweep for clues and saw that the left rear door of the car was open.

They were about to leave for Bible School.

When I arrived on the scenery, the boy greeted me with his broad smile and open arms. "Hi Hankie!" You know, there's a special bupp... excuse me...a special bond between dogs and little boys. It's one of the constants in the universe. When nothing else makes sense, when the rest of the world seems to be falling apart and driven by greed and pettiness, we can always fall back on that special bond between dogs and boys.

I flew into his arms and gave his face a good licking. Sometimes those face-washes will produce a few tasty memories of breakfast, which makes the dog's job quite a bit more interesting, but this time we drew a blank—no traces of toast, jelly, bacon or...I was fixing to say "eggs," but we'll skip that.

The point is that someone, either Little Alfred or his mom, had done some scrubbing on his face and had removed all traces of breakfast, but that was okay. In this life, love and devotion are way more important than jelly.

The boy seemed excited about going to Bible School. "We're learning about Joseph and his coat of many colors."

Joseph? I did a search on that name and got one result: Joe Fred. Remember him? He was the grasshopper who'd had the starring role in Drover's miserable little song. Was this some kind of clue? I didn't think so.

Alfred continued. "And Noah's ark and Zacchaeus up in the tree."

Zacchaeus must have been a cat, which reminded me: our local cat needed to be parked in a tree, and I would attend to that just as soon as Sally May departed the ranch.

The boy's eyes were shining. "Hankie, maybe

you could go to Bible School with us."

With us? Did that include his mother? Ha ha. That would never happen. Sorry.

I was glad to see my pal excited, and I sure didn't want to stomp on his idea, but as far as me going to town...well, that didn't sound very practical. I went to Slow Caring Wags on the tail section, to let him know that I appreciated the invitation.

He looked into my face and smiled, and you know, that kid had the sweetest smile. Sometimes his grin showed an ornery streak, but this time... just innocence and little-boy sweetness, and he said, "Hankie, I wish you'd go with me. The other kids would love it. You'd be the star!"

The star? Me? No kidding? Wow, what could I say?

Hey, I don't go around trying to make a big deal out of myself, but...the star, huh? I had to admit it was kind of an interesting idea. How many dogs get a chance to be the star of anything? Very few.

One of the things that comes with the title of Head of Ranch Security...and this is something we have to cope with...one of the things that comes with the so-forth is that, well, a lot of people and dogs see us as something special, out of the ordinary, a kind of celebrity...even a star.

Yes, it was a pretty interesting idea, but...

The lad tossed a glance toward the house and lowered his voice. "I don't think my mom would mind."

Oh? I wasn't so sure about that. I mean, Sally May was pretty particular about who got to ride in her car and I couldn't remember ever being invited. Also, we'd had some, uh, tension in the relationship that very morning.

A twinkle came into his eyes. "She doesn't have to know."

Yeah, well, there was a little problem with "she doesn't have to know." His mother had several Mommy Sensing Devices that included radar for dogs and X-ray vision for little boys, and somehow she always seemed to know everything about everything.

"You could hide on the floor in the back. It could be our very own secret."

Hmmm. I hadn't thought of that, hiding on the floor, beyond the reach of Mommy Radar. That was pretty clever.

"Please, Hankie? Please, please, pleeeeeeze!"

You know, a lot of dogs don't pay attention to the bupp...excuse me, to the kids, and consider them little nuisances. I guess if those mutts had their way, they'd choose to live in a world without messes and noise and all the other stuff that comes with kids.

But let me tell you something about cowdogs. *We care about the children.* When they're in danger, we're ready to rumble. When they're unhappy, we're unhappy. When they're having a bad day, we're having a bad day. When they cry, we cry. And when they go to town...

I get a little choked up, just talking about this stuff. I mean, the burp of loyalty between a boy and his dog is so powerful, it actually shorts out the rational mind. For a few moments in time, we can't think of anything except keeping a smile shining on the faces of our little pals.

And think about this. One day, Alfred would grow up and none of this would be important to him, but now, today, he wanted to share his life and experiences with me. Even more touching, he wanted to share ME with the less fortunate children of Twitchell.

Would I volunteer for this mission? Yes. Of course. Absolutely. Wild horses couldn't drag me away. Anything for the kids!

I communicated these thoughts through ears, eyes, tail wags, and a loud bark, and we sealed the deal with a hug.

But then...uh oh. We heard sounds coming from the house. The door opened and closed. Footsteps swished on the sidewalk. The yard gate squeaked. Sally May was coming.

I looked at the boy and he looked at me. He whispered, "Quick, in the car!"

Roger that!

I dived into the car and assumed a Stealth Position on the floor. Alfred dived in right behind me, slammed the door shut, and became a statue of The Perfect Little Boy: good posture, hands clasped in his lap, eyes straight ahead, a smile stamped on his mouth, and his feet on the floor.

Actually, his feet were on top of me, but that was okay. Anything for the kids.

Sally May settled Baby Molly into her car seat, closed the door, and walked around the back of the car. Then...gulp...the sound of her feet on the gravel stopped. She was looking into the left rear window. I squeezed my eyes shut and hoped...

"Oh, there you are. Ready to go?"

In a stiff, unnatural voice, the kid said, "Yes, Mother, all set to go."

She entered the car and closed the door. "When did you start saying, 'Yes, Mother'? It almost makes me...well, I appreciate that I didn't have to go looking for you. We're already running late." She twisted the rear view mirror and looked at her face. "The idiot."

"What's wrong, Mom?"

"Your dog bashed me in the face and I'm getting a black eye. I tried to cover it with make-up, but it still shows."

The boy's mouth dropped open and we exchanged a look of, well, alarm. The thought had just struck him that...uh...taking me to Bible School might not be such a great idea, not today, not with all the, uh, bad feelings and so forth.

He swallowed hard. "Hey Mom, I need to tell you something."

"Not now, sweetie, we're already late."

She started the car and we went ripping away from the house. You can always tell when she's "running late." Tires spin and gravel flies. Dogs, cats, and chickens had better get out of the way.

Borp.

Good grief, I was sealed inside an automobile, swaying back and forth, racing toward town, and something scary was going on in my gizzardly depths. Remember that rotten egg? I remembered it. And you know what else? There's a condition called "car sickness." It's caused by the rocking motion of a vehicle, and made worse when the vehicle is warm and stuffy.

By the time we reached the highway, the air inside the car seemed very warm and very stuffy. I pushed myself up to a standing position and glanced around, looking for...I don't know what, a door, an exit, an open window, anything that would allow me to escape this...

Uh oh.

My head began moving up and down. I had been through this before and knew what it meant. Powerful, unseen forces had taken control of my body.

Ump. Ump. Ump.

Little Alfred's eyes almost popped out of his head. "Hankie, no!"

I gave him a Tragic Look. Sorry.

"Hey Mom, you need to stop!"

"Stop?"

"Hank's back here...and he's fixing to throw up!"

"Hank? Oh my word! No, please, not today!"

"Hurry, Mom!"

She must have heard my "umps" and figured out that this was no joke. She pulled off the highway and hit the brakes.

"Alfred Leroy, *how did that dog get in my car?*"

The boy stared straight ahead and shook his head, and tears began flowing down his cheeks. "I don't know, Mom." He burst out crying.

Well, I felt bad for the boy, but a whole lot worse about the convulsions in my stomach. I mean, we're talking about an explosion in the boiler room, big-time trouble.

She got the car shut down, dived outside, and jerked open Alfred's door. "Hank, out, quick, hurry!"

You know, if she'd pulled over just five seconds sooner, we might have...I mean, it all happened so fast. I leaped out of the car, but the damage had already...it lay on the floor.

She leaned into the car and stared at the, uh, material on the floor. "Green?" At that same moment, she caught a whiff of it and...this is really painful. The sound that leaped out of her mouth was something between a shriek and a squeak. "Aaaah! What is that? Alfred, honey, get out of the car. Hurry, and don't breathe the fumes!"

She gagged, clapped a hand over her mouth, and jerked her son out of the car, then ran around to the other side and rescued Baby Molly.

And there we stood, a homeless family on the side of the highway. The car had become an abandoned, contaminated, toxic, radioactive piece of junk. Alfred wailed and boo-hooed. Sally May tried to console him, while holding Molly, shaking her head, rolling her eyes, and muttering dark syllables under her breath.

I felt terrible. Actually, I felt quite a bit better, physically speaking, but I'm talking about the emotional burden of the so-forth. I couldn't help feeling that, well, I had been partly responsible. In fact, I felt such a rush of sorrow, I was about to lick Sally May on the ankles, but a tiny voice inside my mind whispered, "*Don't do that.*"

Good advice. I skipped the Ankle Wash and slithered under the car.

So there we were, stranded and adrift on the endless plains of the Texas Panhandle. The silence was terrifying. At last, Alfred said, "What do we do now, Mom?"

"I don't know. What was that dog doing in my car?"

"I wanted him to go to Bible School."

"You wanted...how could you do this to your own mother!"

They both seemed on the virgil of tears, but just then, we heard the sound a vehicle approaching. It slowed down and pulled off the highway. It stopped. Two doors opened and closed. Footsteps approached. I dared to peek out and saw...holy smokes, it was Loper and Slim, and halleluiah for that!

CHAPTER NINE

Big Trouble

They walked up to the car and glanced around. Loper said, "Hi, Hon. What happened to your eye?" This brought a poisonous silence, broken only by Alfred's sniffles and the sounds of Sally May about to...well, either burst out crying or explode. Loper and Slim exchanged glances. "What's going on here?"

The flood gates opened and out it came. The turkeys. The collision between my head and her eye. Late to Bible School. A dog in the back seat. And the unfortunate incident that had brought us to this awkward moment—the Poisoned Egg Event.

She wrapped it up by saying, "I have a black eye, my car is ruined, and I'm late to my Bible

School class!" Loper and Slim burst out laughing. Her eyes flamed. "AND IT'S NOT FUNNY!"

Loper went to her and gave her a hug. "Hon, I know it's not funny, but it really is. Look, nobody's hurt. We didn't have an earthquake or a hurricane or a car wreck, and everything's going to work out fine. I'll take you and the kids to town in my pickup. You'll be a little late, but God will understand."

At last she managed to squeeze up a little smile. "Well, I hope He does. But my car smells horrible. I don't know what that dog ate..."

"Not a problem, hon, don't give it a thought. Slim can drive it back to the ranch and give it the full treatment." He turned to Slim and said, "In this time of crisis, I need to be with my family."

Slim gave him a frigid glare. "Yeah, and you're a low-down skunk."

Loper winked. "Be happy in your work. And don't forget to take the dog."

The family seemed to be in a better mood when they climbed into the pickup, but Slim wasn't anywhere close to being in a good mood. When the pickup pulled onto the highway and sped off to town, he glared after it with smoldering eyes, and yelled—this is an exact quote—he yelled, "I hired onto this outfit as a cowboy.

Nobody said anything about cleaning up dog drool!"

Boy, he was really steamed. He stood there for a moment, boiling and fuming, then saw a paper cup on the side of the road. He stomped over to it and kicked it with all his might.

It was a great kick. His right leg went high in the air. The cup crunched and flew all the way across the ditch. The sad part was that Slim put so much passion into wrecking the cup, he pulled the hamster muscle in the back of his thigh. The hamstring muscle, I guess it should be, and it must have hurt like crazy.

He let out a howl, grabbed his leg with both hands, bent over like a turkey, and started hopping around. Well, I hadn't planned on putting in appearance this soon, but what's a dog to do? We're loyal to the little children, and we're loyal to our cowboy companions. Cowdogs and cowboys go together like...I don't know, like nitro and glycerin, I suppose. Or like salt and pepper. Or bacon and eggs.

Forget the bacon and eggs.

The point is that my cowboy had wounded himself, and never mind that he'd done it in a display of childish, bone-headed behavior. One of the reasons dogs get along so well with cowboys

is that...well, we understand childish, bone-headed behavior. You might even say...never mind.

So would I leave the safety of my position under the car and rush out to give comfort to my cowboy companion? You bet I would! I rushed out to give him aid and comfort, and it wasn't my fault that he tripped over me. He had eyes. I was just trying to...

"Get away from me!"

Fine. If he wanted to hop around like a one-legged goose on the side of a major highway and bring disgrace to every member of our ranch community, it was no skin off my nose. Let him make a spectacle of himself.

You know, the relationship between cowboys and their dogs has been exaggerated. A lot of times, when they do silly things, we would rather not be associated with them.

I slithered back under the car and watched him limp and moan. At first, it seemed merely childish and bizarre, but it turned funny when the driver of a passing car saw the drama...and stopped.

It was Chief Deputy Kile of the Ochiltree County Sheriff's Department. He got out of his squad car and walked toward Slim. "What's wrong? You hurt?"

Slim hobbled over to the car and leaned against it. "I kicked a paper cup and pulled a hamstring." Deputy Kile waited for the rest of the story. "Never mind. Stick your head inside the car and take a deep breath."

Deputy Kile did that...and jumped back. "What is that?"

Slim straightened up and tested his leg. "Bozo barfed on the way to town and Loper stuck me with the job of cleaning it up."

The deputy laughed. "Oh. Well, I'll see you around." He started back to his car.

"Coward! Wait! Are you carrying a shovel?"

"Yes, but it needs an operator."

"Bobby, it's so sad, what's happened to this country. Nobody cares about anybody but theirselves. Here I am, injured on the side of the road..."

"I'll loan you the shovel, but I want it back, clean." He fetched a small, square-blade shovel out of the trunk of his car and handed it to Slim.

He snatched it. "In America, people used to help their friends and neighbors."

"Yep, but that was long ago."

Slim went to work on the, uh, cleaning project, and this seemed a good time for me to say hello to

Deputy Kile. You know, there's always been a bond between cowdogs and law enforcement officers. In many ways, we're involved in the same line of work, don't you see. I crept out from beneath the car and gave the deputy a friendly smile.

"Hello, Hank." He reached down and rubbed me on the ears. "How's it going, buddy?" From inside the car, we heard a series of odd sounds. It appeared that Slim was, well, gagging on the fumes. The deputy chuckled. "It's awful noisy out here, isn't it? Used to be, the countryside was quiet and peaceful, but any more..."

Slim dashed around to the back side of the car and...gee, what was he doing? His voice fractured the silence. "Earl!"

Deputy Kile cackled. "Any more, you can't find peace and quiet, even in the country. If it's not an airplane making noise, it's a cattle truck or some cowpuncher throwing up on the side of the highway."

Slim returned, looking a bit pale. "That dog ate a rotten egg!"

"I've got a HAZMAT suit in the trunk."

Slim gave him a scorching glare. "Bobby, Baxter Black's a comedian. You ain't even close. Stick with what you do best, although I can't think of what that might be."

The deputy chirped a laugh. "Well, try to hold down the noise. Me and Hank have things to talk about." Slim went back to his job, and the deputy and I continued our conversation. "So how's everything at the ranch, Hank? Have you eaten any good eggs lately?"

"Earl!"

We had a nice visit, Deputy Kile and I, in spite of all the noise. At last Slim finished the job, cleaned the shovel with dirt, and handed it back to the officer.

"Thanks for nothing."

The deputy reached into his shirt pocket and handed Slim a business card. "We're here to serve. Call me any time, day or night."

Whistling a tune, Deputy Kile walked back to his car. Slim glared after him. "Bobby, the citizens of this county get to vote on the sheriff. Tell your boss that he just lost the cowboy vote, and it was all your doing!"

The deputy waved goodbye and drove off. Slim glared down at me. "Well, I got rid of one pain in the neck, but I've still got you. Get in, and you can ride in the back with what's left of your breakfast."

Gee, what a grouch. Fine. I could ride in the

back with my so-called breakfast. He had scooped out the worst of it, so I figured...gasp, arg! It still smelled awful back there, but Slim rolled down all the windows and it was bearable, much better than sitting up in the front seat with the man I had thought was my friend-to-the-end. Obviously, I had been misinformed about that.

But sitting alone in the back seat didn't spare me from Slim's weird sense of humor. You know what he did? Oh brother. See, the man thinks he's a songbird, a famous singer who's missed his chance to be famous, so he makes up these corny songs, and guess who has to listen to them.

The dogs.

He sings them when we're trapped inside a vehicle and can't jump out, so we have to sit there and suffer through them.

Can you believe a grown man would make up a song called "Don't Haul a Sick Dog in the Back of Your Car"? Well, you can believe it or not, but I'm here to tell you that he *did*. I know, because I had to listen to the whole thing.

I'm sure you wouldn't want to hear it. I mean, it was so childish and dumb! Oh well, I guess it wouldn't hurt to let you listen to it. Hang on.

Don't Haul a Sick Dog In the
Back of Your Car

When the dog throwed up on the way to town,
Everybody inside rolled the winders down.
If he'd done it in winter, they might have been
doomed,
From frostbite if not from the poisonous fumes.

When they seen his lunch on the back seat floor,
The passengers tried to jump out the doors.
But the doors wouldn't open and they couldn't
get out.
It's a wonder they didn't just faint and pass out.

Sing yodel-ee-lay-hoo and yodel-ee-yip.
Old Hankie sure knows how to mess up a trip.
The doors wouldn't open, they couldn't get out.
It's a wonder they didn't just faint and
pass out.

Most usually when puppy dogs barf in a car,
It don't smell any worse than a lousy cigar.
But Hankie ate eggs that were rotten, and stunk.
They smelled 'bout as nice as a decomposed
skunk.

What made it so tragic, not funny at all,
Is the driver was trying to answer the call
To teach little kids at the Methodist Church,
But the dog throwing up put her job in the lurch.

> Sing yodel-ee-lay-hoo and yodel-ee-yip.
> Old Hankie sure knows how to mess up a trip.
> She was 'spose to teach kids at the
>   Methodist Church,
> But the dog throwing up put her job in the
>   lurch.

The family was stranded, the car was a wreck.
Sally May muttered something 'bout wringing
      his neck.
But then a brave cowboy relieved her distress.
Like Hoppy and Roy, he cleaned up the mess.

This song has a lesson for volunteer moms
Who are teaching the kids about Proverbs and
      Psalms.
Your day will go better and seem less bizarre,
If you don't haul sick dogs in the back of your car.

> Sing yodel-ee-lay-hoo and yodel-ee-yip.
> Old Hankie sure knows how to mess up a trip.
> Your day will go better and seem less

bizarre,
If you don't haul sick dogs in the back of
    your car.

Don't haul a sick dog in the back of your car.

So there you are. I told you it was a silly little
nothing of a song. Furthermore, it was a pack of
lies. He wasn't even with us in the car, so he
couldn't have known what went on. And did you
notice the part about the "brave cowboy" showing
up and saving the day? What a joke. Bravery
had nothing to do with it. He cleaned up the
mess because the boss MADE HIM, and he
whined and complained every step of the way.

Now you know what I have to put up with on
this ranch.

It was so sad, the way things had turned out,
friend against friend, neighbor against neighbor.
And you know what really broke my heart?
Everyone on the ranch was mad at ME, but I
hadn't done anything wrong. Honest. I had
fallen victim to a whole series of...

Wait. I almost said that I had fallen victim to
a whole series of bad-luck events, but let's take a
closer look at that. Let's examine the whole

concept of "luck." Pay close attention, because you're fixing to learn that I had been pulled into a deep, dark conspiracy that involved...well, you'll see.

CHAPTER TEN

The Charlie Conspiracy

Okay, here we go.

Your ordinary mutts explain their lives in terms of good luck and bad luck. Those of us in the Security Business have moved far beyond such shallow thinking. To put it into simple terms, we don't believe in luck at all. So-called "good luck" comes from our wise decisions and intelligent behavior. So-called "bad luck" is actually...this will probably surprise you, I mean, it's a pretty sweeping concept..."bad luck" is actually the work of our enemies.

Yes, our enemies, and I'm talking about the ones we rarely see, the ones who are working day and night to underwear our undermine. I'm talking about the Charlies. They come in many different forms and disguises: spies, secret agents, night monsters, and alien creatures from another planet. They've even been known to dress up in chicken suits. They are clever beyond our wildest dreams and they never sleep.

Obviously, this was the work of the Charlies and they had struck me a deadly blow. Somehow, they had penetrated our systems and had made evil use of the cat, the turkeys, a hateful fly, Drover, and even Little Alfred.

Are you beginning to see a pattern here? It was the Charlies *who had planted the poisoned eggs in the barn.* Yes, they planted the eggs, knowing that I have a terrible weakness for slurps...for eggs, even as we speak.

Which is a little weird. After a guy has been poisoned, you'd think...never mind.

So there you are, a little insight into the shadowy world we face in the Security Business. Now you know why we seldom sleep and why we sometimes bark all night. The Charlies are out there in the darkness. Never doubt it.

Slim Chance didn't understand any of this. He lived a simple life as a bachelor cowboy, never dreaming what might be going on behind his back, and there was no way I could explain it.

We made our trip to the ranch in frosty silence, he driving the car and me in the back seat, breathing the lingering vapors of a vicious plot. Riding in the back was okay with me. I had nothing to say to him, nor did I want to hear any more of his tiresome music.

Oh, he did find an opportunity to make one last smart remark. When he pulled up behind the house and shut off the car, he looked back at me and said, "Like I've always said, pooch, you sure have a way with the women."

Very funny.

He opened the back door and let me out. Since he'd already messed up his hamster muscle, he wasn't able to deliver a boot to my tail section, although I'm sure that's what he wanted to do. What a grouch.

No wonder the American cowboy is a vanishing breed. Nobody can stand to be around them, not even their dogs.

I hung around to make sure Slim did a proper job of cleaning up the mess in Sally May's car. I have to admit that he did okay. I mean, he actually went to the house and fetched a bucket of hot water, and he actually added *soap* to the water. And, forgive me if I faint from surprise, he actually scrubbed the carpet with a sponge.

I was shocked. I mean, I'd always supposed the guy had an allergy to soap and water, but here he was...what a low-down dirty trick! You know what he did?

I'm not going to tell you.

All right, I'll tell if you promise not to laugh, because it was NOT funny.

Okay, I was sitting there, supervising, maybe twenty feet west of the car. When he'd finished scrubbing, he opened all the doors to let the car air out, picked up his bucket of water, and started walking north.

I saw nothing unusual or alarming about this skinnerio. It appeared that the man was going to dispose of the dirty water, just as you would expect, and pitch it out into the weeds. His eyes were directed straight ahead, to the north, and he wasn't looking at me, didn't even know I was there—I thought.

The next thing I knew...SPLAT! He nailed me with a bucket of dirty water, and we're talking about drenched. I jumped two feet straight up in the air, I mean, I thought the Charlies had crept out of the bushes and...I don't know, drilled me with a death ray or something.

It was an ambush, plain and simple, and Old Trusting Hank never saw it coming, never

suspected a thing.

I heard the roar of his laughter and saw him doubled over with his hands on his knees, and he yelled, "There, by grabs, that makes us even!"

That's what I have to put up with around here. Just when you think those guys are doing serious work and have stopped goofing off, they come at you with some twisted trick and...phooey.

By the way, I got soap in my left eye and it stang. Is that the correct word? I'm pretty particular about using correct language, and do you know why? The children.

Ring, rang, rung.

Ting, tang, tongue.

Sting, stang, stung.

Okay, that checks out. I got soap in my left eye and it stang.

Anyway, Slim enjoyed his little moment of triumph, and laughed all the way up to the machine shed, where he continued a job he'd been working on for several days: repairing sickle blades on the hay mower. See, our hay crop had been a disaster, because of the drought, so Loper had decided that they would mow and bale the grass and weeds that grew in the ditches along the county road. As he said, "In a bad drought, you bale up anything that can't run and hide."

I didn't go along with Slim or help him replace the sickle blades. To be honest, I had lost all interest in his projects on the ranch. I know that sounds harsh, because...well, think about it. When the dogs get discouraged and lose interest, it says bad things about the future of the ranch.

No kidding. Hey, you hear stories all the time about ranches that grind to a halt and go up for sale. You know what's behind those sad stories? *The dogs have lost interest and stopped caring*, and most of the time you can trace it back to some thoughtless, careless event, such as a cowboy pitching mop water on the Head of Ranch Security.

They just don't realize...oh well. Slim was on his own, and if the ranch fell apart, he would have to take full responsibility for it. A dog can only do so much.

I was in the midst of these thoughts when... you know, sometimes you get the feeling that you're being watched. Have you ever experienced such a feeling? It came over me all at once. I *knew* I was being watched, and naturally my first thought was that the Charlies had returned.

I whirled around and did a Full 360 Scan with visual instruments. It revealed no Charlies, just a...can you guess? A cat. I caught sight of his head in the iris patch, two ears perked straight up in the air and a pair of cunning yellow eyes that were staring at me.

I was being spied upon by Pete the Barncat. That's always annoying, but on this particular occasion, I found myself yielding to a wicked grin. Heh heh. See, Kitty's missile defense shield had gone to Bible School, and now it was just me and him, all alone, on a ranch far from town.

Pay-backs. It was time for some serious pay-backs.

I turned and made a "careless stroll" down to the yard gate. There, I stopped. "Hey Pete, how's it going, pal?"

His annoying kitty voice reached my ears. "Well, well, the hero has returned! You left in the car with Sally May and returned in the car with Slim. I'm sure there's a story behind that."

"I'm sure there is, but you'll never hear it."

"And the bucket of water?"

"Oh, you saw that too."

"I try to stay alert, Hankie."

"How nice. Well, since you're so alert, perhaps you noticed that Sally May isn't here, Kitty, and you probably know what's coming next."

"Hmm, let me think. Does it have something to do with a tree?"

"No, much worse."

"So...you're feeling bitter about the Turkey Debacle?"

"Cute name. Yes, I'm feeling very bitter about all your slimy tricks, but before we go plunging into violence and bloodshed, I need to get something straight."

"Oh goodie. Should I come out and join you?"

"Whatever you think. It won't change anything, but come on."

He crept out of the iris patch and rubbed his way down the fence, until he was sitting only two feet in front of me, with the fence between us. "There. Now we can talk."

"One thing, Pete, I need one piece of information to wrap up this case." I tossed glances over both shoulders and leaned toward him. "That deal with the turkeys...were you acting alone or was it something bigger? I must know. Were you working for the Charlies?"

He gave me a blank stare. "You'll have to help me with that, Hankie. Who are the Charlies?"

"The Charlie Monsters, my mortal enemies. They've been trying to take over this ranch for years. They're masters of disguise. They work mostly at night, but sometimes they show up in the daytime, and we never know what form they might take."

"Hmmm, the Charlies. Let me think."

"Hurry up."

His mouth dropped open and he gasped. "Wait! I remember now. Yes! The mailman!"

That word sent a tingle of backbone down my electricity. Holy smokes, it appeared that I was about to break this case wide open...and it involved a suspect I'd been watching for years!

CHAPTER ELEVEN

The Plot
Plottens

I began pacing, as I often do when all the pieces of the puzzle begin falling into place. "You were recruited by the mailman? Ha! I knew it! I've had that guy under cerveza for years. I knew he was up to no good."

"But Hankie, I had no idea…"

"Of course you didn't. The Charlies never leave tracks or clues. They're clever beyond our wildest dreams. Okay, Pete, we're on to something big. Just a few more questions. Were the turkeys in on it too?"

"Oh yes. He trained them. You didn't notice?"

"I missed it, Pete, completely missed it. I had no idea this was going on right under my nose." I paced over to him. "Last question: the rotten eggs."

He looked up at the sky. "That's not exactly a question, Hankie, so you'll need to help me on that one too."

"Right, sorry. Did the guy in the mailman disguise plant three rotten eggs in the machine shed, knowing that I might very well eat them?"

"Oh, *those* rotten eggs! Yes, yes. Three of them, correct?"

"Exactly. We're on the same page. So it *was* the mailman! Oh, what a sneak!"

"I wondered what he was doing in there, but I never dreamed...Hankie, you didn't eat them, did you?"

"Only one, and let me tell you, it turned me wrong-side out."

"Bad?"

"Real bad, right on the floor of Sally May's car."

The cat uttered an odd squeak and turned away. "I am so hee hee!"

"You're what?"

"I'm saddened, Hankie. I'm sure it made things worse with Sally May-hee."

"You can't even imagine. She was livid...and who could blame her? She was on her way to teach Bible School when the tragedy occurred."

He turned to me with…well, you'd have to call it a look of admiration. "It was such a huge conspiracy, Hankie, so dark and twisted, but you've managed to figure it out all by yourself!"

I walked over to him. "That's what we're trained to do, Pete, but I have to admit that your tip about the mailman was helpful."

"Thank you, Hankie."

"It wasn't huge, but it helped." There was a moment of silence. "On the other hand, Kitty, you were involved in a plot that got me in deep trouble with Sally May, twice, and we can't ignore it."

"Hmmm. What do you suggest?"

I paced away from him and pondered this big decision. "Tell you what. It's too hot for us to be running around and scuffling in the yard. Pick out a tree, climb it, I'll bark a few times, and we'll call it good. What do you think?"

A smile bloomed on his mouth. "I think that's brilliant, a perfect solution. Off I go."

He scampered away, climbed that big hackberry tree in the southwest corner of the yard, and sat down on the first big limb. "Ready when you are."

"Ten-four." I leaped over the fence, took up a position at the base of the tree, and delivered three stern barks. "There, let that be a lesson to you. Are you sorry that you allowed yourself to be duped by the Charlies?"

"I am, Hankie, and I must say, this is a touching moment."

"What do you mean?"

"Well, this is the first time we've ever worked together on a case. It's almost as though we've become…friends."

I glanced over my shoulders, just to be sure that we weren't being watched. "Let's don't get carried away. I still have a reputation to worry about."

"Oh, that's right. I won't tell a soul." He stared down at me for a long time, swinging his tail back and forth. He seemed to be in a thoughtful mood. "Hankie, I just had the weirdest idea. I'm going to tell you something that will help you with Sally May."

For a moment, I was speechless, then burst out laughing. "Ha ha. That will never work, Kitty. Even if you came up with a good idea—which I sincerely doubt—I wouldn't believe it. I'd think it was another of your sneaky tricks."

"I see what you mean. Our years of fussing and fighting have done a lot of damage."

"Exactly right, and don't forget all your lying and cheating."

He nodded. "You're right, it was a bad idea. Well, run along."

"Don't tell me what to do."

"Sorry."

"I'm going to run along. This has been fun, but I have to get back to the real world." I whirled around and marched away. I had gone, oh, eight or nine steps...okay, five steps...when I did an about-face and returned to the tree. "I guess it wouldn't hurt to hear this crazy idea of yours."

He was licking his left front paw and didn't even look at me. "No."

"What did you say?"

"No."

I was kind of surprised by what a strong effect that word had on me. I mean, my ears jumped up, my eyes popped open, and my jaw dropped several inches. "Hey Pete, there's something you need to know about me. I hate being told 'no' by a cat."

"No."

The hair on the back of my neck began to rise. "Tell me your idea."

"No."

"One last time, you little creep. Tell me your idea, and be quick about it!"

"No. No, no, and no again."

All at once, the world turned red and a growl began to thunder deep inside my throatalary region. "Okay, pal, that did it. You have pushed me over the edge." I began loosening up the muscles in my enormous shoulders. "And here's what's fixing to happen. Tell me your idea or *I will chew down the tree*! This is not a drill."

Heh. That got his attention. He looked as though he'd stuck his tail into a light socket. "You wouldn't!"

"I would. I will."

"You'd actually do that?"

"Correct. Out with it, what's your idea?"

Boy, you talk about a cat that was shook up! He was shaking and gasping, I mean could hardly draw a breath, but at last he was able to speak. "Very well, Hankie. I guess I have no choice."

"Exactly right. Hurry up."

He took his sweet time, but at last he came clean. "When you and Sally May left for town, a cow came out of the brush and walked straight to the garden."

"Hold it right there. Red cow with horns? Orange tag in her left ear with #35 on it?"

"Yes, but how did you know?"

"Ha. That's the notorious Phantom Cow, and we've been watching her for months. Go on."

"Well, she walked up to the garden fence and looked at all the green vegetables. I got the impression that she was about to jump the fence and eat the garden, but just then, you and Slim drove up and she ran back into the brush."

I began pacing. "Of course! That's why she showed up all of a sudden. Don't you get it? First the rabbits, then the deer, and now the Phantom Cow. They all want to eat Sally May's garden, and they're all working for the Charlies!" I whirled around and gave the cat a triumphant smile. "If I can keep the cow from destroying the garden, I'll win big points with Sally May!"

Pete heaved a sigh. "Yes, that was my idea, Hankie. You've dragged it out of me"

I marched back to the tree and glared up at him. "Nice try, Kitty, but your so-called idea is old news. We've been working this case for weeks and were just waiting for the right moment to activate the Special Crimes Unit."

"Oh really. Then I'm sure you know," he fluttered his eyelids, "that the cow just jumped the fence and is eating the garden…as we speak."

HUH?

To be honest, I wasn't…see, the cat was up in the tree and had a much broader field of…fellers, it was time to Launch All Dogs!

"Thanks for the tip, Pete. It wasn't much, but one of these days, maybe we can find a little job for you in the Security Division."

"Oh, thank you, Hankie!"

Wow, what an interrogation! I had extracted vital information from the cat, and now it was time to put it to work. I fired up engines one and two, and went roaring up to the machine shed. I wasn't one bit afraid of that Phantom Cow, but... okay, I was afraid of the old hag. Hey, she'd been recruited by the Charlies and I needed Cowboy Backup.

I cut the engines, coasted into the barn, and sent out a blast of Three Alarm Barking. Only then did I realize that I had blundered into an extremely dangerous situation. What I saw...do I dare describe this? I guess I will, but hang on to something solid.

What I saw in the machine shed sent a cold chill through my entire body: A REAL-LIVE CHARLIE MONSTER WAS CROUCHED IN FRONT OF A CAMPFIRE, COOKING HIS LUNCH!

It was one of the Robot Charlies, the kind with only one eye. They come from another galaxy— the Charlies do, not the eyes. Well, I guess the eyes do too, but never mind.

Suddenly my head swirled with clues and facts that came at me like a load of buckshot.

- The Charlies had launched a full-scale, two-pronged invasion.
- The Phantom Cow had invaded the garden.
- One of the Robot Charlies had captured the machine shed.
- Slim had vanished.
- And, good grief, maybe that's what the Robot Charlie was cooking over his fire—the remains of poor Slim!

This was awful.

Well, I had already announced myself with the Three Alarm Barking, and there was no turning back. The Robot Charlie heard me. He raised up from his campfire, turned around, and glared at me with that horrible Cyclops eye in the middle of his face.

I won't try to sugar-coat this. The sight of that one-eyed creature chilled my giver and lizard... my liver and gizzard, let us say. I couldn't move, I couldn't bark, I couldn't do anything but stare into the depths of that horrible eye. And then...

CHAPTER TWELVE

Incredible Finish, Just Incredible

Holy smokes, I almost fainted with relief. Whew! You won't...ha ha...you won't believe this. It was Slim Chance, welding on the hay mower and wearing a welding hood! Ha ha. In other words, there was no Robot Charlie cooking Slim's remains over a bed of coals.

Wow. If I'd had more time, I would have...I don't know, laughed or celebrated or something, but don't forget that we had been invaded. We didn't have a moment to gain. I looked directly into Slim's eyes (he had removed the welding hood, and that really helped) and gave him a suite of barking techniques that delivered a complex message:

"Slim, over the years you and I have done

more than our share of goofing off, but we must put that behind us. This is a new day, a new deal. The Phantom Cow is in Sally May's garden and, buddy, I need your help."

To be honest, I had my doubts that he would get the message. I mean, this was the same guy who sang corny songs and threw mop water on his dogs. But you know what? Something about the tone of my barking penetrated all the Goof-Off layers of his mind, and he seemed to understand that something was wrong.

He shut off the welder and set the hood on the floor. "Okay, pooch, I'll bite. What did you find, a rattlesnake?"

No, not a snake, much worse. Let's go!

As you know, Slim was not an Olympic sprinter. He moved at his own pace, which varied between slow and slower, but by George, he came.

I went streaking down the hill, set up a forward position outside the garden, and began laying down a withering barrage of Mortar Barks. The Phantom Cow was having a dandy old time, munching squash blossoms. She heard me, of course, raised her head and gave me fierce look that said something like, "Buzz off, doggie."

Would I take that kind of lip off a cow that was trespassing in our garden? Uh...yes. I mean, bravery is very important in this line of work, but we must spend it wisely, so to speak.

I would wait for Slim. Someone needed to open the gate, right? And if we had to send troops into the garden, Slim was more qualified than I to, uh, lead us into combat. No kidding. But I would be right behind him.

It took him forever to get there, but he finally made it, limping because of his hamster muscle. He recognized the cow right away. "Good honk, it's that old rip that stays off by herself. Okay, pooch, I'll open the gate, and you let her have it." He swung the gate open and pointed inside. "Go get 'er!"

I gave him a blank stare that said, "Me? Forget that. You go get 'er."

He shook his head and muttered "Bozo" under his breath. Staying outside the fence, he walked around to the back side of the garden and waved his arms at the cow. "Hyah, go on, get out of there!"

I knew what he was doing and agreed that it was the right strategy: stay outside the fence and shoo her out the gate. The only trouble was, it didn't work. Instead of running away, the cow turned and faced him as he walked around the fence. She wasn't afraid of him and she had no intention of leaving.

Slim looked at me. "Hank, squirt in there and give her the treatment."

Give her the treatment? Ha. No thanks.

"Chicken liver. Okay, by grabs, Plan B." He glanced around and found a limb that had fallen from one of the elm trees. He broke it off so that it was just the right size for a club, and limped back to the gate.

I was there, waiting for orders, and gave him Loyal Wags on the tail section. He curled his lip at me. "You know why she didn't go out the gate?"

Uh…no. Why?

"Because you were standing in it."

Oh.

"Mister Barf In The Car."

Did we need to bring that up again? Make one little mistake around here…

"Come on. If she's hard of hearing, you might have to break with tradition and do some work."

He gets so childish sometimes.

He entered the garden and I…well, pretty muchly stayed behind him and kept him between me and the cow. It was just a precaution. Don't forget, that cow was working for the Charlies, and we had every reason to suppose that she might have some dirty tricks.

Slim stayed close to the fence and walked around behind her. He got himself in the right position to run her out the gate, but she didn't turn toward the gate. She continued to face him, glaring, swishing her tail and shaking her horns.

This wasn't looking good. Slim picked up a dirt clod and nailed her between the eyes. The cow bawled, shook her head, and took a step toward him. He raised the club.

"Now listen, you old bat, leave the garden, or me and you are fixing to have a collision. Hank, you ready?"

Sort of. Maybe. Sure.

He moved toward her and waved the club. "Hyah! Scat!"

Any normal cow would have turned and trotted out the gate. This was not a normal cow. Instead of leaving, she dropped her head and charged. Slim gave her a whack on the head, but she didn't even notice. She got him loaded on her horns and pitched him into a spot between the okra and the black-eyed peas.

Well! It was obvious that we needed to pull our troops back to a fresh position outside the garden. I mean, this was a bad cow and somebody could get hurt. I whirled around and headed for the gate.

"Hank! Help!"

I stopped in my tracks. You know, there are certain words that resonate in a dog's mind, and one of them is "help," especially when it's called out in a desperate tone of voice by one of our friends.

I'll be frank. It isn't a word we yearn to hear, but when it comes, it shuts down our main circuits and throws everything over into the Emergency System. At that point, everything is automated. We don't THINK. We DO.

And what I did surprised everyone in the garden—Slim, me, and especially the Phantom Cow. I hit Turbos, sprinted through the tomatoes, launched myself into the air, and grabbed a mouthful of her left flank. That got her attention. She bawled, bucked, snorted, twisted, whirled around, and tried to hook me with a horn.

Foolish cow. She missed with the horn and I took a bite on her left ear. Bad idea. See, when they toss their head, if you're clinging to an ear, you get air-mailed. I got air-mailed into the fence, but it gave Slim enough time to get back on his feet. He jerked off his leather belt and gave it a twirl. When the cow turned on him, he laid the heavy buckle between her horns.

WHACK!

That got her attention, and I went roaring back into the fight, biting anything that didn't bite me back—flanks, nose, heels, tail, ears. Oh, you should have seen us! Slim gave her a thrashing with his belt and I took what was left.

Fellers, that cow might have thought she was tough when she got there, but after we'd worked on her for a while, she changed her mind. She lost her taste for fresh vegetables and quit the garden.

A sane cow would have gone through the open gate, right? I mean, that's why we'd opened it. But in one last hateful gesture, she plowed through the south fence and headed for the brush along the creek. But by George, she was gone.

Slim placed his hands on his knees and gasped for air, and I did a little gasping too. When his head came up, he was wearing a grin. "Pooch, we won, just like John Wayne cleaning out the saloon."

Absolutely. Who?

"And we saved most of the garden. I've got a feeling that you might have salvaged some of your reputation."

Salvaged...oh yes. Sally May.

"And I'll even volunteer to be a character witness. That don't happen very often around here. Good dog."

He gave me rubs and pats, then we went to work, rebuilding the fence, which was quite a wreck. We had just finished stretching up the last strand of wire when Sally May and Loper came back from town.

Slim laid down his fence stretchers and gave me a wink. "Let's go speak to the authorities."

Gulp. Okay, but I was feeling a little uneasy about this.

On the way up to the house, I switched over to the Contrition Program: low head, low tail, sad ears, downcast eyes. And I did some rehearsing on my story: "Sally May, I know you might find this hard to believe, but I was poisoned by the Charlie Monsters. It was all part of a huge conspiracy. The turkeys were in on it, the cow, your cat...and the mailman is actually a secret agent! Honest. No kidding."

Would it work? I wasn't hopeful. But you know what? It turned out better than I could have dreamed. Sally May's mood had softened since I'd seen her on the side of the highway, and let me see if I can sort it all out.

First of all, the black eye hadn't turned as dark as she'd feared, and at Bible School, it had become the Story of the Day. Second, Slim had succeeded in restoring her car to its original condition, clean and fresh, so she didn't have to burn it or push it over a cliff. That did a lot to improve her mood.

And third—this was the Big One—Slim Chance gave a ripping-good testimonial about our skirmish with the Phantom Cow. "Old Hank barked the warning and backed me up when she came after me. I hate to say it, but he might have saved me and your garden both."

This next part will blow you away. Sally May was so impressed, she invited me into her yard and we sat down on the porch, just the two of us. I wasn't sure where this was going, but when I saw the warmth in her eyes, I had a feeling that it was going to be okay.

She spoke in a soft voice. "The Good Book says, 'Ask now the beasts and they shall teach you.' You keep trying to teach me that this isn't a perfect world. Thank you for the lesson. I'll try to be more patient, but Hank...please try to be a good dog."

Oh, yes ma'am. I swore an oath, took a pledge. No more Bad Dog for me!

She pulled me into a hug. "Oh my word, you need a bath!"

What? Hey, Slim had already given me a

bath, a whole bucket of soapy water. How clean does a dog have to be?

Oh well. I got a bath, right there in Sally May's yard, and it wasn't so bad. The important thing is that Sally May and I had patched things up, and I embarked on a new campaign to become the Dog of Her Dreams.

Pretty amazing finish, huh? You bet. I had turned back an invasion of the Charlie Monsters and had won a huge victory over the...I almost said, "over the cat," but one thing bothered me.

Was there any chance that Pete had...I know this sounds crazy...was there any chance that he'd done me a *favor* behind my back? Tricked me into doing...surely not. I mean, he's just a dumb little ranch cat.

Never mind. This case is closed.

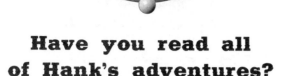

Have you read all
of Hank's adventures?

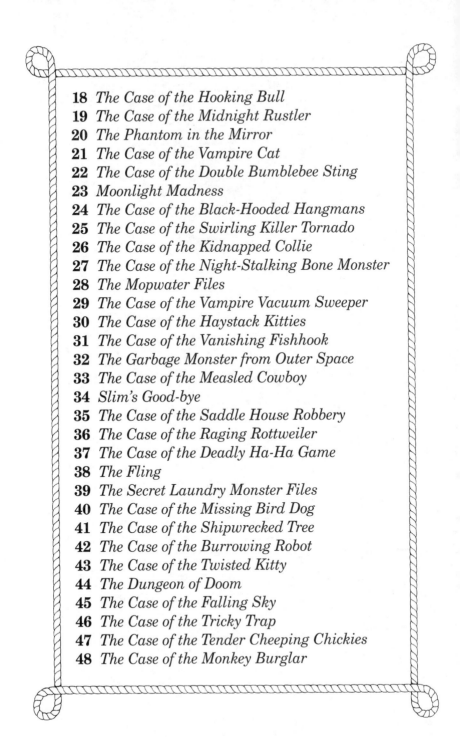

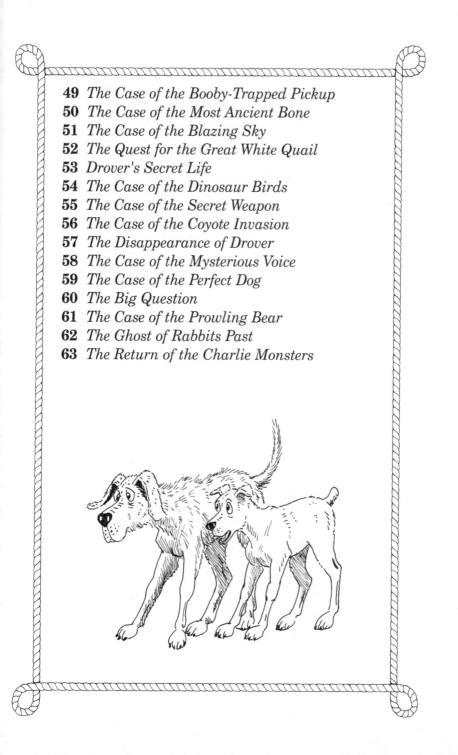

Join Hank the Cowdog's Security Force

Are you a big Hank the Cowdog fan? Then you'll want to join Hank's Security Force! Here is some of the neat stuff you will receive:

Welcome Package
- A Hank paperback
- An Original (19"x25") Hank Poster
- A Hank bookmark

Eight digital issues of
***The Hank Times* with**
- Lots of great games and puzzles
- Stories about Hank and his friends
- Special previews of future books
- Fun contests

More Security Force Benefits
- Special discounts on Hank books, audios, and more
- Special Members-Only section on website

Total value of the Welcome Package and *The Hank Times* is $23.99. However, your two-year membership is **only $7.99** plus $5.00 for shipping and handling.

☐ Yes I want to join Hank's Security Force. Enclosed is $12.99 ($7.99 + $5.00 for shipping and handling) for my **two-year membership**. [Make check payable to Maverick Books.]

Which book would you like to receive in your Welcome Package? (#   ) any book except #50

BOY or GIRL

YOUR NAME   (CIRCLE ONE)

MAILING ADDRESS

CITY   STATE   ZIP

TELEPHONE   BIRTH DATE

E-MAIL   (required for digital Hank Times)

Send check or money order for $12.99 to:

Hank's Security Force
Maverick Books
PO Box 549
Perryton, Texas 79070

DO NOT SEND CASH. NO CREDIT CARDS ACCEPTED.
Allow 2–3 weeks for delivery.
Offer is subject to change.

The following activity is a sample from *The Hank Times*, the official newspaper of Hank's Security Force. Please do not write on this page unless this is your book. Even then, why not just find a scrap of paper?

For more games and activities like this one, as well as up-to-date news about upcoming Hank books, be sure to check out Hank's official website at **www.hankthecowdog.com**!

"Photogenic" Memory Quiz

We all know that Hank has a "photogenic" memory—being aware of your surroundings is an important quality for a Head of Ranch Security. Now you can test your powers of observation.

How good is your memory? Look at the illustration on page 5 and try to remember as many things about it as possible. Then turn back to this page and see how many questions you can answer.

1. Was Hank looking to HIS *Left* or *Right*?

2. How many rails were on the fence? *3, 4*, or *none*?

3. Which foot was Hank scratching with? HIS *Front Left, Back Right*, or *Back Left?*

4. What was on the plant? *A Praying Mantis? A Grasshopper?* Or *A Paying Mantis*?

5. Was the gas nozzle pointing to the *Left* or *Right* in the picture?

6. How many of Drover's eyes were open? *0, 1, 2*, or *all 3*?

John R. Erickson, a former cowboy, has written numerous books for both children and adults and is best known for his acclaimed *Hank the Cowdog* series. He lives and works on his ranch in Perryton, Texas, with his family.

Gerald L. Holmes has illustrated numerous cartoons and textbooks in addition to the *Hank the Cowdog* series. He lives in Perryton, Texas.